ALSO BY
DARCY COATES

The Haunting of Ashburn House
The Haunting of Blackwood House
The House Next Door
Craven Manor
The Haunting of Rookward House
The Carrow Haunt
Hunted
The Folcroft Ghosts
The Haunting of Gillespie House
Dead Lake
Parasite
Quarter to Midnight
Small Horrors

House of Shadows
House of Shadows
House of Secrets

Black Winter
Voices in the Snow
Secrets in the Dark

THE
FOLCROFT
GHOSTS

DARCY COATES

Poisoned Pen
PRESS

Published by Poisoned Pen Press, an imprint of Sourcebooks
P.O. Box 4410, Naperville, Illinois 60567-4410
(630) 961-3900
sourcebooks.com

The Folcroft Ghosts was originally self-published in 2017 by Black Owl Books. "Sub Basement" and "Crypt" were originally self-published in the short-story collection *Quarter to Midnight* in 2015 by Black Owl Books.

Library of Congress Cataloging-in-Publication Data

Names: Coates, Darcy, author.
Title: Folcroft ghosts / Darcy Coates.
Description: Naperville, IL : Poisoned Pen Press, [2020]
Identifiers: LCCN 2019056945 | (trade paperback)
Subjects: LCSH: Paranormal fiction. | Domestic fiction. | GSAFD: Ghost
  stories.
Classification: LCC PR9619.4.C628 F65 2020 | DDC 823/.92--dc23
LC record available at https://lccn.loc.gov/2019056945

Printed and bound in the United States of America.
VP 10 9 8 7 6 5 4 3 2 1

CONTENTS

THE FOLCROFT GHOSTS

CHAPTER 1
TEMPORARY

SPECKS OF RAIN HIT the windshield and evaporated within seconds. It had been a clear, warm day when Tara and Kyle stepped into Mrs. Jennings's car outside Plymouth Hospital, but the farther they drove, the worse the weather became. Coastal trees slowly gave way to heavier, thicker mountain growth, and the wide paved roads were swapped for twisting dirt trails.

"It will probably only be for a couple of days, anyhow." Mrs. Jennings took a bend slightly too fast, and Tara braced herself against the door. "Just long enough for a fun little visit."

"Yeah." Tara stared at the knotted pine trees shifting past the window. Her brother had dipped out of the conversation by keeping his attention fixed on the book in his lap. Not for the first time, Tara wished she could read in the car without becoming sick.

"I'm sure they'll be lovely. They seemed very excited when

they called." Mrs. Jennings drummed her fingers on the steering wheel and snuck a glance at Tara in the rear-view mirror. Her voice had a bright, energetic lilt, but a quiver belied the carefree words.

Tara tried to return the older woman's smile. She knew Mrs. Jennings was trying her best. She'd already let Tara and Kyle stay in her too-small house with her own children the previous night, and she was spending nearly a full day driving them to their grandparents'.

Mrs. Jennings cleared her throat. "And when your mother's out of the hospital, I'll bring lots of precooked meals so she doesn't have to worry about food."

When, not *if*. Everyone was being so optimistic. But Tara couldn't think about her mother without seeing the ghost-gray, slack face with the incubator tube strapped to her mouth, artificial breaths filling her lungs, and the body that was unresponsive when the doctors prodded at it.

Mrs. Jennings licked her lips. "You know I wish you could stay with us. But we've had this holiday booked for months…" She quickly added, "And the house is being fumigated anyway, so even if we canceled—"

"I know. Don't worry." Tara tried again to smile, but the muscles in her face weren't obeying her. "You've been really generous."

Mrs. Jennings was all but sweating guilt. Tara couldn't understand why; their families were friends, but not very close ones. She was lucky if they saw each other twice a month. But Mrs.

Jennings had been the only person to visit when their mother was admitted to the hospital, and more because of proximity than merit, she'd taken on the role of surrogate mother.

And now we're being passed to our grandparents.

It would be her first time meeting May and Peter Folcroft. Her mother had talked about them only once, when Tara had asked. Her mother had said they lived a long way away and didn't keep in touch. Tara was surprised they'd volunteered to take her and her brother.

Tara glanced at Kyle. He was small for an eleven-year-old, and his hair was overdue for a cut. He kept his eyes fixed on the book, but he hadn't turned a page in several minutes.

"I think..." Mrs. Jennings squinted at a wooden letter box jutting out by a narrow driveway. "I think this might be it. Yes, good, number forty-eight. Isn't this pretty!"

Giant shaggy trees lined the driveway. Unlike the coast's manicured gardens and neatly spaced palm trees, the mountain property's plants had been allowed to grow wherever and however they liked. Maples, oaks, pines, and liquid ambers grew scattered about the area, sometimes so close together that they strangled each other. Vines and shrubs tangled through the gaps between the trunks, and late-season wildflowers created splashes of color.

Mrs. Jennings's four-wheel-drive car, which had only ever seen suburban roads, lurched over the winding driveway's bumps and potholes. Kyle looked up from his book to scan the area with a quick glance then raised the novel higher to block out the view.

Tara understood. For him, a fantasy world was easier to cope with than their new reality.

The driveway seemed to stretch on forever. When it finally opened into a clearing, Mrs. Jennings made an appreciative "ooh" noise. "This is lovely. I'm sure you kids will have so much fun here. Look, there's even a swing."

Tara twisted to see the wooden board suspended from a great oak near the front of the house. Shifting in the breeze, it looked old enough to be from her mother's time. On their other side, an angular concrete structure rose out of the ground, partially hidden by a copse of trees. Tara thought she saw the outline of a door.

The two-story house built of stone and wood stood a little apart from the surrounding forest. The mountain rose up behind it, blocking out much of the late-afternoon sun, and leaves littered its sharply peaked roof. Tara strained to see the two figures standing in front of the house, but shadows hid their faces.

Mrs. Jennings swung the car around the circular driveway and pulled up near the house's front. Her voice was bordering on unnaturally eager as she said, "Here we are, kids. Let's get you unpacked."

Kyle pretended not to hear, so Tara kicked his leg when Mrs. Jennings wasn't looking. "C'mon," she whispered. "Be polite."

He frowned but closed his book and slid out of the car. Mrs. Jennings popped open the trunk and pulled out their suitcases, leaving Tara and Kyle to face their grandparents.

"Hello." The woman, May, stepped forward first.

Tara was surprised; when she'd heard her grandparents lived on a rural property, she'd pictured weather-hardened, stout people. But May looked closer to a grandmother in a Hallmark ad. Her long, silky gray hair had been tied into a bun with a blue ribbon that matched her checked dress and white apron. Her face was heavily wrinkled, but the creases all seemed to fall in the right way and bunched up around her sparkling eyes when she smiled.

"You must be Tara," she said then nodded to the boy hiding behind Tara. "And Kyle. I'm so, so happy to finally meet you."

"Hi." Tara swallowed, unsure of what she was supposed to do or say to give a good impression. "Thanks for having us."

"Ooh, poor thing." May pulled Tara into a hug. She smelled like cinnamon, and the unguarded affection, so different from the distanced pity the nurses and even Mrs. Jennings had offered, made Tara's throat tighten. May withdrew just far enough to include Kyle in her hug, then she patted both of their backs. "I can't tell you how sorry I am. But you're welcome to stay with Peter and me for however long you need to. Come in. I baked a cake; I hope you like apples."

Her husband, Peter, extended a hand first to Tara then Kyle. He was taller and gaunter than his wife but dressed neatly in jeans and a button-up shirt. His smiles were more guarded and his handshake brief, but there wasn't any of the reluctance or irritation Tara had been dreading. He gave them both a gruff "Welcome" then took the suitcases from Mrs. Jennings.

"Come in," May continued, gently guiding them into the house. "You're probably tired from the drive. I have your rooms made up, but I hope you'll join us for a chat. I've been looking forward to meeting you for so, so long."

Mrs. Jennings followed them as far as the doorway then shrugged to adjust her cardigan. "Would you like me to stay for a bit, kids?"

May beamed at her. "You're very welcome to join us for some tea, but it's getting late. I'd worry if you were driving home in the dark."

"Oh, yes." Mrs. Jennings frowned slightly as she glanced at the sky. "I suppose… Will you be okay from here, kids?"

Kyle kept his eyes fixed on the wooden floor, so Tara spoke for both of them. "Yeah. Thank you. For everything."

"Of course, of course. Couldn't leave you kids fending for yourselves." Mrs. Jennings edged toward the door. "You've got my number. Call me if you need anything. I'll keep an eye on your house, too, take a loop past it during the school run to make sure everything's okay."

"Thanks."

Mrs. Jennings gave a final tight-lipped smile, waved, then hurried back to the car. Tara had the impression that she was glad to be gone—her duty was done, and she could get home and focus on her own family again without guilt.

As the engine revved, Tara turned back to face her grandparents and the building that was going to be her home for the foreseeable future.

CHAPTER 2
ROOMS FOR TWO

"WHAT DO YOU LIKE to drink?" May clasped her hands together as she smiled at Tara and Kyle. "You might be a little young for coffee, but I have hot chocolate, tea, milkshakes… I even bought some of that soda teens seem to like."

"Luggage first," Peter said. "You'll have plenty of time to feed them later, May."

Tara moved forward to pick up her suitcase, but Peter had already lifted both. "I've got it," he grunted and nodded toward the stairs at the back of the hallway.

A small tug on her jacket made Tara look over her shoulder. Kyle had grabbed the hem and was holding it as he followed. He hadn't done that in years.

The narrow staircase groaned, but Peter moved up it with a speed that belied his age. At the top, he turned down the hallway and stopped in front of a door. "Here's yours," he said to Tara. "It used to be your mother's."

The hinges creaked as the door opened. The room wasn't large, but it was clean and welcoming. A colorful quilt added life to the otherwise-plain room, and the window overlooked the forest behind the house. Peter put her suitcase at the base of her bed then led them back down the hallway. They passed the door next to Tara's and stopped at the last room down the hallway.

"Yours," Peter said, squinting at Kyle over Tara's shoulder.

Kyle nodded mutely but didn't look inside as Peter placed the suitcase at the bed's foot. Peter's gray eyes tightened slightly as he peered at Kyle. "What's the matter? You're not mute, are you?"

Tara bristled. "No, he just gets shy around new people."

"Hmm." Peter shut the door. He examined them for a second, shrugged, and turned back to the staircase. "I guess it's better to say nothing than risk saying too much. Let's get you some of that cake."

The man's tone hadn't held any hostility, and Tara relaxed a fraction. As Peter went down the stairs ahead of them, she whispered to Kyle, "Try to be friendly. They seem nice."

He didn't answer but kept hold of her jacket.

As Tara followed the stairs to the ground floor, she ran her hand along the wooden wall. The house felt old, as though the passing years had made it heavier. Every floorboard groaned, and the glass panes in the windows had warped. It was clean, though, if a little cluttered.

May was shedding her apron as they entered the kitchen. A

frosted cake took up the center of the white-clothed dining table, surrounded by plates and cups, a vase of flowers, and two parcels wrapped in brown paper and string.

"I didn't know what drink to make," May said as she hurried to pull out two seats. "So I made three types of tea. There's spiced fruit juice and soda, too, or I can make you something else."

Tara slipped into one of the seats. "Any kind of tea's good for me, but Kyle might want the soda."

"Oh, good. I asked the store manager to give me whichever type is most popular. If you don't like it, you can blame him."

For the first time since the police officers had knocked on their door, Tara laughed. May flitted around like a humming-bird, pouring their drinks and cutting cake, while Peter reclined at the head of the table and blew on his mug of coffee.

"We really are glad you could visit." May finally settled into her seat opposite the siblings, her long fingers tracing invisible patterns on the tablecloth. "Despite the circumstances."

"It's a shame we couldn't come before," Tara said. She tried the cake then went back for another spoonful. "You have a really lovely house."

May beamed. "Thank you. Peter's parents built it close to… well, eighty years ago, I suppose. It's held up well."

"Got a lake out back," Peter said. "I'll take you fishing sometime."

Kyle peeked up from his plate. He'd been asking their mother to take him fishing for years, but their mother, Chris, had always said it was too expensive or too far to travel.

"I can't believe how quickly time passes." May's eyes were shining as she looked between them. "You turned fifteen a few months ago, didn't you, Tara? And you're nearly twelve, Kyle? We really should have visited a long time ago—been a bigger part of your lives—but your mother…well…" She shifted forward, a hint of nervousness tainting her smile, and picked up the paper-wrapped shapes. "We can be a family now. Here, we bought you some presents."

Tara dropped her spoon to take the parcel, equal parts surprised and touched. She slipped the string tie off and unwrapped the paper.

"I hope you like it," May said.

"Oh—yes! Thank you!" Inside the parcel was a small Polaroid camera. Tara grinned as she turned it over. "This is really cool."

She looked toward Kyle and found him holding a fantasy novel. May had found his weakness, and his face brightened as he read the blurb. "Thanks." It was the first time he'd spoken all day.

May bit her lip to hide a grin as she glanced at Peter, and he gave her a lazy smile in response. "May picked them out for you."

"I'm glad. It was so hard to guess what you might like," she said, rising to clear away their plates. "I'm sure you two must be hungry. I'll make a start on dinner. Settle in, and feel free to have a look around. I'll call you down when we're ready to eat."

Kyle trailed after Tara as she climbed the stairs. He held two books close to his chest—the novel he'd brought for the car ride and May's gift. Tara crossed to his room at the end of the hallway and went to the window to look over the lawn below. "You doing okay?"

"Yeah." He placed the books on his bedside table, lining them up parallel to the edge, then sat on his bed. "You're right. They seem nice. But I still wish we could've stayed at home."

Tara turned back to the room. Not for the first time, she wondered how different things might have been if a nurse hadn't realized they didn't have a father and if Mrs. Jennings hadn't visited the hospital. She didn't even know what happened in situations where minors were left without a guardian. Kyle insisted they were put in foster homes, but she wasn't sure how much of that was real knowledge and how much was fiction from his books.

"Cool presents," Kyle said, nodding to the novel. "I haven't read this one yet. And you can take pictures for that awful drama blog of yours."

She rolled her eyes. "It's not a drama blog. It's a blog that contains drama. Ve-e-e-ery big difference."

"It's an echo chamber." He was mimicking both their mother's voice and words. "And an excuse for antisocial behavior."

She laughed, but the silence that followed felt hopelessly empty.

"Is Mum going to be okay?" Kyle asked.

It was the first time they'd had a chance to talk privately since arriving at the hospital. Uncertain how to answer, Tara returned to looking out the window. "The doctors say she will."

"But even if she comes out of the coma, there could be brain damage, memory loss, physical impairment—"

"Stop it." Tara's tone was harsher than she'd intended. Kyle was probing for reassurance from the only remaining person he trusted, and Tara wished she could give it to him. But she hadn't understood the hospital notes she'd read, and the doctors had only ever made general, noncommittal statements. Kyle the bookworm probably knew more about their mother's state than she did.

"Things are going to be okay," she said at last. It was the best she could offer, even though she knew it was horribly inadequate for both of them. "Remember what Mrs. Jennings said. Worrying won't help Mum. We just need to look out for ourselves for a couple of days while she rests."

Kyle stood and opened his suitcase. He began hanging up the four identical shirts with robotic precision, and Tara knew she'd frightened him back into his shell.

"I mean it. We'll be okay."

"You should unpack. Don't want to leave it too late."

Tara sighed. "Okay. You know where to find me." She gave his hair a ruffle on the way past then stepped back into the hallway.

Even with four people in it, the house felt strangely empty. She counted the doors up and down the hall. The house would easily accommodate ten people; compared to their old apartment, the Folcrofts' home was a mansion. But the air felt still, and although noises echoed from the kitchen below, the upper level seemed too quiet. Tara moved to her room with quick steps and released a held breath as she crossed the threshold. She closed the door and turned back to the space that was supposed to be hers.

The suitcase lay on its side. Tara frowned, put her new camera on the dressing table, and picked up the suitcase. She'd seen Peter place it on its end, she was sure.

She set it upright again, tilted her head, and waited to see if it fell. It didn't. She nudged it with her foot—first in one direction then the other. It didn't even rock.

Weird. She looked toward the closed door. *Was someone up here while I was talking to Kyle? I didn't hear anyone, but then, I wasn't listening…*

A shudder ran up her back. She snatched the suitcase off the ground, laid it on the bed, and opened it to unpack. Her wardrobe was a little more varied than her brother's, but still basic and embarrassingly outdated. Before the accident, she had an allowance and a part-time job at a fast-food outlet but was using her earnings to save up for a new computer. Kyle had good grounds to tease her about her blog, but Tara didn't care. She'd grown an immense network of friends through it. On the internet, no one cared how she spoke, what clique she fit into, or whether her jeans ended two inches above her ankles. She was proud to be a part of the misfits.

Tara finished her unpacking quickly then shoved the suitcase under her bed. She flopped back on the quilt and stared at the wooden ceiling. Peter had said the room had once been her mother's. *How many times must she have looked at the same patterns in the boards?* Then the idea occurred that the ceiling might be hers for the next three years, until she was old enough to move out. Her throat tightened. She rolled off the bed, returned to the hallway, then turned to the stairs. Company—even awkward company—was better than being alone.

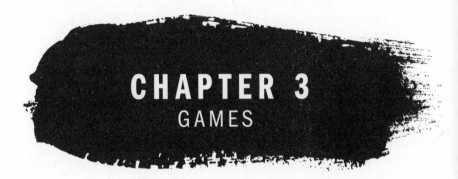

CHAPTER 3
GAMES

MAY AND PETER WERE speaking in hushed tones as they washed the dishes but startled as Tara entered, giving her the impression they'd been talking about her.

Shifting on her feet, Tara rubbed at her forearm. "Can I help with anything?"

"You're such a sweet girl." May dried her hands on her towel and flipped it over her shoulder. "We were just finishing up dinner. Would you like to set the table? Cutlery is in this drawer here."

Tara opened the indicated drawer and fished out four knives and forks. "Sorry, this is a weird question, but did either of you go into my room a little earlier?"

May tilted her head to one side as she strained vegetables. "No, honey. Why do you ask?"

"Oh. Just—my suitcase was knocked over. I'm trying to figure out how it happened."

"Sorry, yes, that was my fault." May chuckled and moved the empty pans into the sink. "I went to check the window was closed. I must have kicked it over. So sorry."

Tara frowned. *Why did she say she hadn't been in there when I first asked?*

"You'll find this is an old house," May continued. "Lots of creaks. Lots of breezes. It might take a few days to adjust to its quirks. But it's built solidly, and it has a lot of love in it. I hope you and Kyle will be happy here."

"Thanks." Not knowing what else to say, she hovered by the tableside while May ferried a small roast into its center. Peter disappeared up the stairs to call Kyle, and May nodded toward an empty chair.

"Settle in and help yourself. The both of you could do with a good feeding. You'll have to tell me your favorite foods, as well. I'm not so good with the modern, foreign kinds, but I can make anything as long as I have a recipe."

Tara caught a glimpse of a stack of ancient cookbooks on a shelf above the fridge. May seemed to prefer classics over experimentation.

Kyle arrived and took his seat at Tara's side, and for a moment, the room was quiet save for the clatter of cutlery as they served themselves.

Then May said, "It's good to have a few more people in the house. It's been just Peter and me for such a long time. The place dwarfs us."

"It is big," Tara agreed. "We spent last night at Mrs. Jennings's and had to share a room with her twins. It's a bit of a system shock to have separate rooms."

"When this house was built, it was nearly bursting. Peter's parents, his aunt and uncle, four siblings, plus eventually, myself. Family has always been very important to us Folcrofts."

Tara wondered if May knew that her daughter had legally changed her surname. From the very brief conversations she'd had with Chris about her grandparents, Tara had gotten the idea that May and Peter weren't interested in seeing their grandchildren. After meeting the couple, though, she saw that was blatantly untrue. That meant there must have been some kind of fallout to create such animosity. She dearly wanted to know what had happened but wasn't sure if it was the best conversation to have during their first night together.

"When was the last time you saw Mum?" She tried to keep her voice light.

May and Peter glanced at each other.

"A very long time, dear. Too long." May hesitated then placed her cutlery back on her plate. "She went through a bit of a rebellious phase. Traveled a lot. We had trouble finding ways to contact her. This was before cell phones, of course. When she did finally settle down, we made contact, but she was busy a lot of the time, the drive was long, and we never seemed able to find the time to meet up."

Tara nodded, but an uncomfortable sensation had settled over her. May's eagerness to explain the prolonged distance left her with the impression that there was more to the story.

"Could I call the hospital after dinner?" Tara kept her eyes on her plate. "Just to see how she's doing."

"Of course, dear. I'll show you where the house phone is."

"Thanks, I can use my cell."

"Oh." May bit her lip. "I'm afraid cell phones don't get reception in this old place. Why don't you give them to me? I'll put them somewhere safe, where they won't get broken."

Tara hesitated, but May was already holding out a hand, so she slid her phone out of her pocket and handed it over.

"Do you have a cell phone, too?" May asked Kyle. His hesitation was enough of an answer for her to extend a hand. "I'll look after it."

May took both phones and put them in a wicker basket on one of the kitchen's higher shelves. She sighed as though pleased and settled back at the table. "Yes, I'm afraid technology doesn't often play nicely with this house. We don't have a TV or a computer because of that."

"Oh." Tara's heart dropped. She'd been counting on her blog to keep her connected with the outside world. Again, the idea that they might need to spend more than a couple of days at the house flashed through her mind, and she bit her lip.

May leaned forward, a nervous smile tugging at her lips. "Is something the matter?"

"She can't survive without the internet," Kyle said, surprising Tara. He shot her a brief, wicked smile, and she scowled in response.

For a second, May's happy expression folded into one of deep worry, then she brightened again. "Oh—there's a computer in town. In the library. I can take you there tomorrow."

"Thank you." Tara was almost ashamed of how relieved she felt at that small allowance.

She finished dinner and, while May and Peter began washing up, fished the hastily scribbled hospital number out of her pocket and went to use the living room's phone.

The call was brief, and most of the time was spent being transferred and put on hold. Chris's condition hadn't changed, but the nurse promised she was taking good care of her.

Tara hung up and turned to find Kyle waiting in the living room's doorway. He must have seen her expression, because he didn't ask any questions. Instead, he nodded toward the kitchen. "May and Peter want to play a board game."

"Sure." Trying to sound happier than she felt, Tara followed her brother back to where the small table had been cleared and an old game Tara didn't recognize was set up.

"How's your mother?" May asked.

"No change."

She made a murmuring, comforting noise and ushered Tara into a chair. "Let's try to take your mind off it for a little while. This is one of my favorite games—I'm sure you'll love it, too."

The game was simple, but Tara found it easy to sink into the moment. Kyle became chattier as his innate ability to calculate probability gave him an advantage. Tara had the impression that both grandparents were deliberately losing, but they looked happy, so she let them get away with it. By the time

Kyle had won the second game by a long margin, it was nearly nine.

"That's bedtime," May said, rising and brushing down her skirt. "We'll have a busy day tomorrow, so get some sleep. Who wants a hot water bottle?"

Kyle sent a pained look toward the clock. "Can't I stay up a bit later?"

"Young boys need lots of sleep. Go on, up you go."

Tara didn't argue. Unlike Kyle, who seemed to become more alert the later it grew, the day had exhausted her. For once, she was grateful for an early bedtime.

May pressed a kiss to both of their foreheads then waved as they climbed the stairs. Tara stopped in at her room to fetch her toothbrush then met Kyle in the bathroom.

"They're so *nice*," he said, squeezing out too much toothpaste. The words almost sounded like a complaint.

Tara laughed. "That's a bad thing?"

"Naw, I just mean—I was expecting to be put up in an attic somewhere and ignored. I wouldn't have minded that. I've got enough books. But they're spending all this time with us and wanting to take us fishing and play games—it's like they want to be our family."

"They *are* our family."

"You know what I mean."

She did. "It's not like they want to replace Mum. If anything, they're probably trying to make up for lost time. Maybe they think this is a chance for reconciliation."

"That's what bothers me. They say they wish they hadn't grown so distant from Mum. So why didn't they visit her in the hospital?"

Tara's hand fell still midbrush. That hadn't occurred to her.

Sensing he'd made a strong point, Kyle continued. "They were so eager for us to stay here, so why didn't they drive down to collect us and visit Mum at the same time? She's their daughter."

Tara shook her head. "Okay, I get what you're saying, but don't build this into a big conspiracy. They're old. They probably didn't want to drive across the country. A lot of old people don't like travel."

"She's their *daughter*." Kyle spat out a mouthful of toothpaste.

"I'm pretty sure there was some kind of falling out. Maybe a lot of old hurts that haven't healed yet. But they're happy we're here, they're looking after us, and they've gone out of their way to make us feel at home. Stuff could be a lot worse."

"I still wish we could've stayed at home," Kyle grumbled.

A door farther down the hallway creaked. Tara's heart skipped a beat. She hoped May and Peter hadn't heard too much of the conversation; she didn't want to give the impression they were ungrateful.

She quickly rinsed her mouth, propped her toothbrush in an empty cup by the sink, and went back to the hallway. She wanted to say something to express her gratitude, but all she could think of was, "Good night, Grandma May. Good night, Grandpa Peter."

Two voices answered as one. "Good night." Then May said, "Sleep well, my dear!"

Tara raised her eyebrows. The voices had come from the ground floor, where she'd last seen her grandparents. *Maybe they hadn't come upstairs, after all? May said it's an old house with lots of breezes. The doors probably move on their own.*

Even so, she felt slightly unsettled as she returned to her bedroom. She shut the door firmly, making sure the latch had caught.

CHAPTER 4
THE HOUSE WAKES AT NIGHT

TARA HELD ON TO a spare pillow as she stared at the ceiling. The little clock on her bedside table said it was after eleven, but she couldn't sleep, no matter how tired she felt.

Animals screamed in the forest. Their shrieks cut through the cooling night air like a knife. They were wildcats, Tara thought, or possibly birds she'd never heard before. Every few minutes, the noise was punctuated by an owl's mournful hoot.

The night was clear, and the half-moon washed her room with light. Her window had curtains, but she didn't want to close them. When she'd been a child, her mother had once read her a story about a man who sat on windowsills during winter nights and peeked through holes in the curtains, and ever since then, she'd been careful to keep her view of the outside unobstructed.

She rolled over to face the window and saw a burst of either birds or bats shoot out of the treetops. The black shapes circled for a moment then descended one by one to dive back into the inky woods.

A door creaked as it opened. Tara tried to guess where the noise had come from, but the house was too disorienting. She listened as light footsteps moved down the hallway and stopped outside her door.

"Tara?" Kyle knocked softly. "Are you awake?"

"Yeah." She rolled out of bed, shivering against the cold air, and opened the door to let him in. His face, pinched and pale, was sweaty despite the chill. She gave him a small smile. "Can't sleep?"

"No. I keep hearing things. Can I stay with you?"

"Sure, come in."

Kyle went to the window, arms wrapped around his flannel-covered torso as he shook. He'd only stopped using a night-light the year before, and he still seemed unusually susceptible to nightmares. Tara thought for a moment then said, "Want to build a fort?"

His eyes brightened. "Can we?"

"As long as we keep quiet, sure." Tara quickly assessed her furniture. There wasn't much, but she could make it work. She slid the thin mattress off the bed frame and laid it flat on the floor with the bedside table on one side and a chair on the other, then draped a quilt over the arrangement to make a cave. Kyle crawled inside while Tara turned her bedside lamp on to give them light.

An animal shrieked in the forest, and Kyle shuddered as he pulled a blanket around himself.

"It's just a cat." Tara sat at her brother's side and pulled her knees up under her chin. "If they frighten you, imagine them as fluffy kittens screaming at the moon. It's not so scary that way."

His pale face cracked into a smile that quickly lapsed. "It's not just that. Did you hear the footsteps? Someone's been walking around the house."

"Might be Peter. I didn't hear him or May go to bed—they might have farm work they need to finish tonight."

He made a noncommittal noise. Something crunched through the woods not far from the window. Tara ruffled Kyle's hair to distract him. "Did you start on your new book?"

"Yeah." Finally, he offered her a real smile. "It's really good. It's about these three different clans warring over a seaport…"

Tara listened as he rambled through the plot. She was always amazed at how quickly he could devour books; he seemed to inhale them more than read them. It made birthdays and Christmases easy, at least—his list of desired titles was always at least three feet long.

It took nearly forty minutes, but Kyle eventually dozed off, curled in a fetal position. Tara made sure he had enough blankets to keep him warm then stretched out and tried to get some rest herself.

Feet moved through leaves below the window. Tara rolled her head in its direction, but her room was on the second floor, so she couldn't see anything. The footsteps passed then returned a moment later, traveling in the opposite direction.

They must have had a lot of work to catch up on. I saw a vegetable garden. I wonder if they have animals, as well? I always wanted to own some chickens.

The footsteps moved past a third time, and uneasiness dug at Tara. It didn't sound like someone who was busy with a task. It sounded like someone who'd become lost. That was impossible, though—there was nowhere to become lost *in.*

She slipped out of their tent, careful not to disturb Kyle, and crept to the window. Tiny crystals of frost had started to grow over the panes. Tara's breath plumed as she leaned nearer the cold glass and peered into the lawn below.

A tall figure walked across the sparse ground. It was a man, but while Peter stood straight and balanced, the figure below had bent shoulders and moved with pained, shuffling steps. Tara frowned and leaned so near the window that the tip of her nose touched the glass.

The man turned, and moonlight caught on his eyes, making them flash. His gaze met Tara's, and fear doused her like water. She scrambled away from the window, not stopping until she was back inside the fortress. Kyle shifted but didn't wake. Tara stayed frozen under the quilt, her eyes fixed on the small part of the window she could see, her breathing frantic and tight.

That wasn't Peter. It couldn't be.

She didn't know what to do. Was she supposed to call for her grandparents? She couldn't confront the stranger herself, could she?

The footsteps passed under the window, faded until they were nearly inaudible, then returned.

Tara took a sharp breath to stabilize herself and crawled out of the tent. She kept her body low so that she wouldn't be visible through the window as she hurried to the door. The handle grated as it turned, and Tara cringed. She shifted into the hallway.

"May?" She kept her voice quiet—it was barely more than a whisper—but May must have heard. Scuffing sounds came from down the hallway, then the door opposite Kyle's room opened.

May's long gray hair hung loose about her shoulders, and her white nightdress seemed to glow in the moonlight. She tilted her head to the side as she smiled. "Is something wrong, honey? Would you like that hot water bottle, after all?"

"No—" Tara hesitated then spread her hands helplessly. "There's someone pacing outside my window."

May's smile dropped a fraction, then she pulled it back into place. "Oh, that would be Peter. I'll go and talk to him."

"I don't think it is." Tara rubbed her hands over the goose bumps on her arms. "It didn't look like him."

"Don't you worry, honey. It's him. Go back to sleep." May gave Tara's shoulder a gentle squeeze on the way past, then she disappeared down the stairs. A moment later, the front door creaked open. May's muffled words drifted through the cold night air.

Tara returned to her room and crept back into the tent. Kyle had rolled over but continued to sleep. Tara huddled at his side as she listened to the muted conversation, then the front door clicked as May returned to the house. The footsteps resumed, moving past the window and toward the forest. Tara squeezed her eyes shut and listened as they faded into the rustling leaves and scraping branches. A wild animal howled, followed by a flurry of wings and a screeching bat. Tara stayed awake for a long time, listening for the footsteps, but they didn't return.

CHAPTER 5
LIBRARY

TARA SLOUCHED IN HER chair, her nose close to her computer screen as she read magic_chihuahua's exposé on the local bakery that allegedly had ties to the mob. It was the fourth in an epic six-part series detailing their shady doings, and Tara was pretty far down the rabbit hole.

At the back of her mind, she knew she would get in trouble if she didn't shut the computer down soon. She had badly neglected homework and was supposed to water the houseplants before her mother got home. But the blog post was too juicy to ignore, even for a moment, and there were already twenty-eight comments...

A sharp knock echoed from the door. Tara startled, thinking that her mother had come home early. But Chris had her own key; she never knocked. Did a neighbor need something? Tara rose and crossed to the door. She passed Kyle lounging on the couch with a book propped above his head, and muttered, "Lazybones."

Something wasn't right, though. She could taste the wrongness before she even reached for the door handle. Unease prickled over her skin, making her hair stand on end. A dull warning in the back of her mind told her not to turn the handle. But she already had. Then the door was opening, and the red-haired police officer was leaning forward and saying, "Tara Kendall?"

Tara gasped as she woke. Sweat coated her, and nausea cramped her stomach. The patterned quilt above her head muted the morning sunlight and served as a reminder that she was no longer at home.

She looked to her side. Kyle was still sleeping, though he'd sprawled out farther. Tara sat up, waited for the frightened nausea to pass, then retrieved her towel from where she'd packed it in the wardrobe. It was early. She hoped she could shower and wash off the cold sweat before anyone else in the family woke.

By the time she'd left the bathroom, the house was busy with noise. Tara followed the sound of voices and clattering utensils into the kitchen, where May was serving up breakfast.

"Good morning, Tara!" The older woman beamed and nodded to a seat. "I hope you like pancakes as much as your brother does."

There weren't just pancakes, Tara saw, but bacon, eggs, sausages, and fried tomatoes. She laughed as she took her seat. "You shouldn't cook so much. You'll spoil us."

May ran a warm hand over Tara's hair as she passed. "Maybe you two need a little spoiling. And you definitely need some feeding. I refuse to have hungry children in my house."

Tara grinned and served herself a big plate. Kyle was already halfway through his, and May hummed as she poured drinks and brought them napkins.

Peter, savoring a mug of coffee, raised his eyebrows at Tara. "I hear I gave you a fright last night."

"Oh." Tara hurried to swallow her mouthful. "So that *was* you. I thought a stranger might have wandered onto the property."

"No, we're not close enough to any other house to be bothered by neighbors. I get arthritis at night and find walking helps it more than anything else."

"Right. Sorry. I didn't mean to disturb you."

He waved away the apology. "You did nothing wrong."

Tara returned to her meal, trying to dismiss the lingering anxiety, but the memory of the twisted, shuffling man was hard to erase. It seemed impossible that Peter could be so straight and relaxed during day and so badly contorted at night.

May chatted through breakfast, talking about how nice the day was, but warning that the forecast said storms were coming. Tara tried to listen, but her mind kept turning to the phone in the sitting room. As soon as May rose to clear away plates, she asked if she could call the hospital.

"Of course, you must be so worried. Go on, I'll take care of this."

Tara dialed the now-familiar number and went through the process of being transferred to the right ward then waiting for the nurse to be paged.

"No change yet," Nurse Mann said. Her voice was slow, deep,

and placid, but no matter how soothing the tone, the news wasn't easy to take. "We'll have a different neurosurgeon in today who'll have a look at her. Call back in the evening, if you like, and we should have an update."

As Tara hung up, she sensed movement behind her. May waited, her eyebrows pulling together in concern. "Is it bad news?"

"It's...not good."

May seemed to understand that Tara didn't want to talk any more than that. She wrapped Tara in a hug then stepped back, cupping Tara's cheek in a wrinkled palm.

"How about we head to town this morning? You can spend time on the computer in the library while I do some shopping."

"Yeah." Tara tried to smile. "I'd like that."

"Can I come?" Kyle hovered in the doorway, his eyes wide.

"I'm afraid the library only has one computer, dear, but if you don't mind sharing—"

"Nah, she can be the nerd. I want to borrow some books."

Tara snickered and poked Kyle's shoulder. "Books are nerdier than blogs."

"No way. *Nothing* beats blogs."

May nudged them both toward the kitchen. "Come on, chatterboxes, get your jackets. We can finish this argument in the car."

The Folcrofts owned a beat-up Jeep that looked older than Tara was. She and Kyle sat in the back while May, dressed up in a hat and floral dress, navigated the vehicle down the narrow, potholed lane and toward the main road. The Jeep might have been older than Mrs. Jennings's car by at least a decade, but it handled the drive much better.

Tara peered into the shrubs and trees as they passed. "Peter said you don't have close neighbors. Does that mean there's no one else in this area?"

"Not for a few kilometers. Most of this part of the mountains is reserve, which means it can't be developed. Only very old properties such as ours are allowed to stay."

"Any bears?" Kyle asked. He was warming up to May, Tara was happy to see.

May laughed. "Not near us. We have cougars, foxes, and snakes, though."

The Jeep sped up as it reached the main road and turned toward town. Tara leaned forward in her seat. "We could hear animals last night. They sounded like screams. That would be the cougars, right?"

"Probably—though foxes scream, as well." May's eyes crinkled with a smile. "The longer you spend here, the better you'll grow at telling them apart."

True to form, Kyle had brought a book with him. It was May's gift, and Tara saw that even though it was a doorstop of a tome, he was making solid progress. She suspected he would finish it that day. The trip to the library had come at a good time.

She watched as wooded areas gradually gave way to properties, then they crossed a bridge and entered a small patch of homes and businesses that probably constituted the town. Tara knew they must have passed it on the drive to the Folcrofts', but it had gone by so fast that she didn't remember it.

May parked in front of a general store and climbed out of the car with surprising agility. She placed a hand on both Tara's and Kyle's shoulders and led them down the strip mall. "I'll show you to the library first, so you can spend some time there while I shop. How long would you like? An hour?"

Kyle's eyes were wide. "As long as you can give us."

She chuckled as they entered a small sandstone building. "All right. An hour and a half, perhaps. I'll come and pick you up."

The building was small, but the library owner had clearly put work into making it a comfortable place. An assortment of mismatched chairs were scattered among equally mismatched shelves, and Tara saw a small discolored computer at the back of the room.

"Afternoon," the woman behind the desk said, and May bobbed her head.

"Good afternoon, Sandy. These are my grandchildren. Would you be kind enough to look after them while I do some shopping?"

Sandy didn't look particularly enthusiastic about that, but she nodded, and May waved as she hitched her purse onto her shoulder and returned to the main street.

Tara and Kyle both made a beeline toward their goals. Kyle disappeared into the fiction section while Tara settled into the ancient wooden seat in front of the computer and woke it up. It was a seriously outdated model that made clunking noises when Tara opened the browser, but that didn't bother her. The blog circle she dominated was text-only and didn't need Java or Flash, so it only took a minute to log in.

Plenty had happened during the last couple of days. Tara chewed on her thumb, trying to prioritize what to start with. Scanning through the new blog posts, she saw the next part of magic_chihuahua's series on her local bakery had been posted. Her stomach twisted, and she scrolled past it.

She didn't know how long it would be before she saw another computer, so she replied to comments directed to her then started a new blog post of her own. That way, if it took her a week or more to log back on, at least her friends would know what was happening.

I hope you like lemonade, because life just gave me a metric butt-ton of lemons.

Tara paused, her fingers hovering over the keyboard. Blogs were about sharing life experiences. In her circle, nothing was off the table—she'd read secrets that could ruin people, confessions that would never be whispered in public, and thoughts that would make a journal blush. And yet, it didn't feel right to write about her mother, limp and covered in mottled bruises, laid out on the crisp white bed sheets.

She sat back, her excitement at returning to her native home squashed, then bit her lip and leaned forward again. It's been a weird couple of days, but the crux of the matter is that my brother and I are now staying at our grandparents'. We've never met them before, and I honestly didn't know much about them until we rocked up at their doorstep yesterday.

Tara typed freely, the words flowing as she wrote about sweet May and gruff-but-friendly Peter, the yowling cougars, the food, and the presents. It was easier to process things in a blog post, she found. Maybe one day she would write about what had happened to her mother. But it was still too soon and too private to share, even with people close to her.

She finished with a promise to post as soon as she could and a caution that it might take a few days. She went back to catching up on her friends' news while she waited to see if she got any comments. It was morning on a weekday, so most of her circle would be in school, but she knew a couple of her friends were stay-at-home mums who liked to chat in the comments section.

"Excuse me."

Tara jumped at the voice behind her. A middle-aged woman with curly blond hair stood a few feet back, a frown creasing her eyes. Tara quickly rose.

"Sorry—sorry—you can have the computer now."

"No, that's okay. Didn't mean to startle you." The woman looked toward the library door then back at Tara, her frown deepening a fraction. "You're staying with May and Peter Folcroft, aren't you?"

"Yeah. I'm her granddaughter."

"Gee." The woman bit her lip, apparently trying to think something through. "Sorry, this is phenomenally rude. I'm Pattie—I run the bakery. They told me you were coming to visit, but I didn't think you'd actually… Anyway. Are things…okay? I mean, are you all ri—"

"Tara!" May's sharp call cut off the disjointed question. Tara looked over Pattie's shoulder and saw May in the library doorway, looking faintly flustered and breathing heavily. She smiled and beckoned to Tara. "We need to leave now."

CHAPTER 6
POLAROID

"OH—OKAY." TARA GLANCED from May and back to Pattie. The woman's expression hardened. She looked like she wanted to say something else but bit her lip and turned toward the shelves.

Tara quickly logged out of her blog account and crossed to where May waited in the doorway. The woman beamed at her then called, "Kyle, are you ready to go?"

He staggered toward them, arms weighted down with nearly a dozen tomes. "Can I get these?"

May laughed. "My, you do like reading, don't you? You'll grow up to be a smart young man. Sandy, he can borrow these books, can't he?"

"He'll need a library card," Sandy said.

May gave the librarian a pleading sort of look. "We're in a bit of a hurry. You know me, Sandy. I'll make sure they all come back."

Sandy sighed and shrugged, and Kyle grinned as Tara took half of his stack. They stepped into the warmer outdoors and followed May back to the Jeep. She waited until they were buckled then turned on the vehicle and began driving back up the twisting road. "I'm sorry I had to take you away early. I realized I left a roast in the oven and need to be back before it burns."

"Yeah, no problem," Tara said.

May beamed. "We can come back again later. Just…I don't want that woman bothering you."

Tara frowned. "Pattie? Who was she?"

"Oh, no one important. She runs the bakery. I beat her in a pound cake competition a long time ago, and she's disliked me ever since." The creases around May's eyes scrunched up as she smiled. "One of those silly, petty hatreds that silly, petty people fall into. Knowing Pattie, she'd either try to interrogate you to dig up dirt on me or try to poison the well by telling you lies. She isn't a kind woman."

"Huh." May had looked breathless and disheveled when she'd interrupted Pattie—almost as though she'd run back to the library. *Is Pattie really so malicious that May doesn't want her around us?*

"Did you find enough books, Kyle?" May asked.

"Oh, yeah. Your library isn't as big as ours, but it's got a bunch of super-obscure books. I haven't even heard of most of these."

Tara peeked at one of the volumes he carried. It looked like a pulp book and was so old that the pages were coming loose. She doubted they would be really *good* books, based on how mass-market they seemed, but that rarely fazed Kyle. She sometimes believed that he would read a phone book if nothing else was left.

They turned in to the shadowed driveway. For someone who seemed so gentle, May was an aggressive driver. The Jeep rocked as it raced over tree roots and potholes before it finally pulled up in the turning bay. Tara glanced up at the house. One of the upstairs curtains fluttered, either from Peter watching them come home or from a breeze.

"It must be time for lunch," May decided, even though it was barely past eleven. "Are sandwiches all right? Or would you like something warmer, like a stew or a soup?"

"Sandwiches are great." Tara slid out of the backseat, wondering what had happened to the roast May had said was in the oven, then picked up an armful of Kyle's books to help him carry them inside.

"I think Peter promised to show you the lake this afternoon." May opened the house's door and stood back to let them in. "Will you be all right amusing yourselves for a bit while I prepare lunch?"

"Definitely." The books were heavy, so Tara made for the staircase while May flitted into the kitchen and shook out her apron. Kyle, still reveling in his books, murmured as he followed her, "What a haul. This will last me at least until next week."

"Ha!" Tara nudged Kyle's bedroom door open with her back and dumped her books onto the bed. "How do you even remember which ones you've read? Don't they blend together after a while?"

"Sure. But what does it matter if I forget a story after a month as long as I enjoy it while I'm reading it?"

"You could be a philosopher. A nerdy philosopher who only knows how to turn pages."

"Better than a nerdy writer who lives in the internet."

"That's fair." Tara snickered as she stretched then glanced through the door to make sure both May and Peter were still downstairs. "Did you see that lady in the library? Pattie?"

"Didn't see her. Heard her, though. What did she want?"

"I don't know. That's just it. May made it sound like she was trying to extract gossip from me, but it didn't seem that way. She looked kind of worried. Like she'd seen something that upset her."

Kyle flopped onto his bed and opened the nearest book. Tara, assuming he'd disengaged from the conversation, turned toward the door, but he stopped her on the threshold.

"If she runs the bakery, what was she doing in the library on a weekday? Wouldn't she be busy cleaning up from breakfast and getting ready for lunch?"

Tara bit her lip. "Could've been her day off."

"Tom from school has an older brother who owns a bakery. He says they don't take days off."

"Don't believe everything you hear at school. I speak from experience—at least eighty percent of it is bald-faced lies."

Kyle snickered, but she could see him sinking into the book, so Tara left and followed the narrow hallway back to her own room.

He's changing. She closed her bedroom door behind her and

gazed at the little blanket fort they'd made. *He was never really outgoing. Neither of us was. But since Mum's accident, he's talking less, making less jokes, spending more time in his books… It's like he doesn't want to live in the real world anymore.*

Am I changing, too? She rubbed her hands over her jeans and circled around the room, searching for something to distract her from her thoughts. The Polaroid camera, May's present, sat on her dresser. Tara took it and flipped it over, checking inside. It held a full pack of film.

She'd tried photography for a stint when she was twelve and had even won an amateur contest with a luckily timed snap of a bird yawning. It had been years since she'd touched a camera, though, and she'd never used a Polaroid.

Some pictures of the farmhouse and its surroundings would add color to her blog, but neither the Folcrofts nor the library had a scanner. *I'll just have to wait until I get home to upload them.* The idea that she might not be leaving the Folcrofts' for a long time threatened again, and she slipped the camera's strap around her neck before maudlin could sink its claws into her. She skipped down the groaning staircase and passed May in the kitchen. "Can I help with lunch?"

"Thank you, Tara, that's very sweet of you." May's smile crinkled her eyes as she spread condiments over bread. "But I'm all right here. Go and have some fun."

Tara nodded and stepped through the front door. A scattering of gray clouds kept the sun from being too warm, so she zipped her jacket up to her chin as she strode across the lawn.

She followed the driveway as far as where the trees opened into the clearing, and turned back to take a picture of the house. The building was old and weathered, but it looked almost regal with the woods rising up the mountain behind it. Tara tried to guess which window belonged to her room and which was Kyle's, but there were too many for her to be sure. She lifted the camera to her eye, made sure she'd framed the building properly, and snapped the picture.

The camera whirred, and a black Polaroid slid out. Tara stared at the square for a moment before remembering she wasn't supposed to get light on it, and slipped it into her pocket to develop. She turned and followed the clearing in a circle around the house. Several narrow, overgrown paths speared into the woods, and Tara made a mental note to see where they went later.

Soft scraping noises came from behind the house, and as Tara rounded the corner, she found the source. Peter dug trenches in the garden. He grunted and nodded as he saw her, and she lifted the camera. "Can I take a picture?"

"Sure."

He didn't stop to pose, so Tara snapped the shutter mid-dig, hoping it would come out all right. She slid the undeveloped Polaroid into her pocket as she approached her grandfather. "Are you planting something?"

"Yep. Potatoes here." He dug the shovel into the ground and leaned on it as he waved a hand across the plot. "Carrots are already planted there. Once it's a bit closer to spring, we'll start on the lettuce and herbs."

"I'd like to try gardening. We never had room at our old place. Just a couple of flowerpots on the porch."

Peter snorted. "I don't see the point in growing what you can't eat. But May likes flowers, so we always keep a few patches around. You can watch them come out in spring."

Tara fidgeted with the camera. "If we get to visit again in spring, sure."

Instead of answering, he stomped his foot into the shovel, digging up a fresh clump of dirt. Tara watched for a moment then continued through the garden, admiring the neatly dug trenches and bare pickets that would hold climbing plants in a few months.

She'd nearly circled around the house when she heard May calling from the porch. "Tara! Peter! Lunch is ready."

May had prepared platters of several kinds of sandwiches—more than the four of them could hope to finish in a meal—along with a pitcher of juice and two new types of soft drink for Kyle.

"I can always make something warm if you prefer." She fussed around them, filling cups and patting Tara's hair before taking her apron off and settling into her own seat. "It's a cold day, after all. And if you want something sweet, I have cookies in the oven. Peter, how's the garden coming along?"

"Good." He chewed on one of the sandwiches and lifted his eyebrows. "Gonna finish the potatoes this afternoon."

"You'll have time to take the kids down to the lake, won't you? You promised you would."

"Yep. We'll go after lunch."

May beamed and patted his hand. "That sounds lovely."

They ate quickly, and Peter stood and pulled on his long jacket. He disappeared into the house while Tara and Kyle washed their hands, and when he returned, he was carrying a long, sleek rifle.

"Wha—" Tara took a reflexive step away from the gun, bumping into Kyle, who'd moved behind her.

Peter snorted, amusement evident in his face. "Don't panic. It's for the cougars, not you."

"Is it…legal?"

"Sure."

He didn't elaborate, and Tara wanted to believe him.

May came up behind them and rubbed warm hands over their shoulders. "You almost never see the cougars, but it's still wise to have some defense when you're in the forest. Don't be afraid. Grandpa Peter knows what he's doing."

"Okay." Tara hoped her voice sounded braver than she felt. She glanced at Kyle and saw he was watching her for cues. She forced a smile for his benefit and squared her shoulders. "Let's go."

CHAPTER 7
THE LAKE

PETER SLUNG THE RIFLE over his shoulder as he led them around the back of the house. His paces were quick and long, and Tara had to jog to keep up. He took them past the vegetable garden and into one of the trails that wove through the woods.

Despite the overcast sky, the pace warmed Tara up quickly, and she tied her jacket around her waist. Peter led them over fallen trees and down steep banks, his long legs making the job look easy, and Tara was breathless by the time the path widened and the ground leveled out.

Birds flitted through the trees, and she could hear their wings rustling and muted, quick calls. The crackle of dry leaves betrayed the presence of something larger and heavier just out of sight, and she was suddenly grateful Peter had brought the rifle. Peter seemed unconcerned by their unseen companion. His face was peaceful, and his breathing deep and even.

"There it is," Kyle hissed.

Tara peered through the thinning trees and saw the sparkle of light on water. The path took a final bend, then they were at the lakeshore. The egg-shaped lake, filled with stunning, crystal-line blue water, stretched toward the mountains. The ridges rose around it, creating a natural bowl, and the water was perfectly still except for when a breeze nudged it.

"It gets fuller when it rains," Peter said. "It's fed by the Calif River, which comes down the mountains. There's about eight different types of fish in it, but only two grow big enough to make a proper meal."

"It's beautiful," Tara murmured. She moved closer to the lake's edge, but a steep embankment separated her from the water.

Peter nodded to their right. "There's a pier down there."

Tara and Kyle exchanged a glance, then they were racing each other to the wooden boards jutting out over the water. Kyle beat her—just barely—and Tara gasped in laughing breaths as she followed him down the dock. Lazy waves created slapping sounds as they hit the pier's supports. Kyle followed it to the end and bent over to peer into the water.

Peter's feet made the weathered boards groan as he followed them. "Can both you kids swim?"

"Sure," Tara said. "We lived near the beach. Mum used to take us there on weekends when she wasn't working."

"You can swim here, too, if you like. Just make sure you tell either May or myself first. It's good to have someone who'll keep an eye out."

"For the cougars?" Kyle asked. "Or are there, like, crocodiles in the water?"

"No crocodiles. Just some leeches." Peter fell quiet for a moment, watching as Tara leaned forward to dip her hand into the water. "My sister and I used to swim down here when we were kids. Anna loved the water. My mother used to say she should have been born with gills. We were all shocked when she drowned."

Tara, not sure she'd heard him right, turned. He stood just behind them. His eyes had taken on a hint of sadness as he stared across the water. "She was eight. We'd finished our chores and had an hour before dinner, so she wanted to go for a swim. I sat right where you are, Kyle, and watched her dive as deep as she could. She went down again and again, pulling up handfuls of seaweed and sometimes little crabs, but then one time, she just didn't come up at all."

Kyle had pulled away from the dock's edge and wrapped his arms around his torso. His eyes were huge as he fixated on the rolling blue that suddenly seemed too deep and too dark.

"We never found her body." Peter exhaled, sounding much older than he looked. "We searched for days, but the lake has currents, and once something's lost in it, you're not likely to find it again."

Tara opened her mouth, but words failed her.

"Sometimes I come down here and talk to her. I like to think she stayed with the lake she loved so much. Like she's a part of it now."

"I want to go home." Kyle's words came out as a whisper, but the air was calm enough that they both heard him clearly.

Peter looked at his grandson, faint surprise touching his expression as though he'd forgotten they were there. "All right." His boots thudded on the pier as he made his way back toward the woods.

Tara held her hand out to Kyle. He took it with a grateful sigh and clung to her as they followed Peter back into the woods.

The walk back was less relaxing than the earlier hike. The birdcalls seemed faintly ominous, and the narrow, winding path felt claustrophobic. Tara was thankful when the trees opened up, and they stepped into the clearing.

"You kids okay from here?" Peter asked. "I'd like to spend some more time at the lake."

Kyle didn't answer, so Tara nodded for him. "Yeah, we're good."

He turned and disappeared back into the trees. Tara watched him go then squeezed Kyle's hand. "He didn't mean to scare you."

Kyle's face had taken on an awful gray-green shade. "I never want to go back there again."

"You don't have to."

He nodded then let Tara lead him back toward the house.

She knew why he was so upset. His imagination was always working, and he would have already relived death by drowning a dozen times since hearing Peter's story about Anna.

Peter didn't realize the effect it would have on Kyle. He probably just thought it was an interesting story—a bit of family history. He couldn't have known that sort of stuff gives Kyle nightmares.

When they stepped through the front door, the house seemed strangely quiet. May had cleaned away their lunch, but Tara couldn't hear her anywhere else in the house. "Want to go upstairs?" she asked.

Kyle nodded.

The air in the stairwell felt stuffy and old. Kyle's hand was clammy, and breathing felt harder than normal. She passed the door to her own room and continued to Kyle's. The bronze handle wouldn't turn. She frowned. "It won't open."

"No, it won't."

Both she and Kyle twitched from shock. May stood at the top of the staircase, hands folded neatly over her maroon-striped dress. She smiled, but her eyes were strangely emotionless. "We can't go into that room. The door swelled and froze shut some years ago. Kyle's room is the next one along."

"Oh—of course. Sorry." Tara had forgotten that Kyle's room wasn't next to hers. She turned, Kyle still clinging to her hand, and led him through the correct door.

Her heart was beating too quickly, and she pressed a hand to her chest to quiet it. May had followed them silently—something Tara hadn't thought was possible on the creaky staircase. Kyle finally released her hand and went to the bed, where he'd arranged his books in a semicircle. He sat in the middle of them, almost as if they created a physical shield, and opened one. Within seconds, he was senseless to the world around him.

Tara didn't want to sit alone in her room, so she crossed to the window instead. The forest behind the house took on a darker ambience when the sunlight faded, and she watched as a cluster of black birds flitted out of the trees, circled, and swooped back into the boughs. She closed her eyes and drew in a series of slow, steady breaths.

May had said the other room's door was jammed shut. That wasn't true, though—Tara had felt the handle catch when she turned it. The door was locked.

Why would she lie about something like that? And what's in the room that she needs to hide it from us?

Tara turned back to Kyle. The furrow between his eyebrows told her he was still upset about the lake, though the books seemed to be doing a good job of distracting him. She sat next to him, picked up a volume with a painted dragon on the cover, and tried to read. Her eyes glazed over before the end of the second page, so she tossed it back onto the bed and flopped onto her back.

Something firm poked at her hip, and Tara felt inside her pocket to find the two Polaroid photos she'd taken before lunch. She pulled them out to see how they'd developed.

The colors were off, but Tara thought they looked cool. She grinned as she looked between the one showing the house and the photo she'd taken of Peter. A blur in the second photo caught her attention, and she squinted as she held it close to her nose. "Hey, Kyle?"

"Mmm?"

"Take a look at this. What does it look like to you?"

He sighed as he pulled his attention away from the page and held out a hand. Tara gave him the photo then pointed to the shape behind Peter's shoulder. Kyle's face scrunched up. "I dunno; looks like you're a rubbish photographer."

"Don't be rude. Doesn't it look like a person? There's the head. That bit would be the shoulder…"

Kyle snorted. "It's a camera glitch." He hesitated, tilted his head to one side, and frowned. "What, do you think it's, like…"

"I don't know what it is. Just that it looks like a person." Tara pulled the photo back her way to reexamine the gray shape. It was smudgy, but it really did give the impression of a tall, thin man standing a few paces behind Peter. "You're probably right. It must be a glitch. Peter was moving when I took the photo, so maybe that blurred part of it."

They both continued to stare at the picture. Kyle worried at his lip. "Those white points would be the eyes. And there's even a fuzzy bit down by Peter's side that looks like a hand… You don't think it could be, like, a ghost, do you?"

Tara snatched the photo back, feeling stupid for scaring Kyle again when he'd already had a bad day. "Nah, just a glitch," she insisted, her tone firm. "I think it looks pretty cool, though."

"Yeah." He smiled, but his face collapsed back into anxiety within a second. "It is."

CHAPTER 8
JOURNAL

"DON'T YOU LIKE COLESLAW, Tara?"

Tara startled at her name. She realized she'd been picking at her food, and managed a smile. "No, no, it's lovely. Thanks, May. Just a lot on my mind."

May made small comforting noises in the back of her throat and ran a hand down Tara's hair. "I know. Everything's so different. It's a lot to take in. But you know your Grandpa Peter and I are here to help. We want you to be happy."

"Thanks." Tara scooped up a forkful of the coleslaw. May had made it and the dressing from scratch. It tasted worlds apart from the store-bought kind her mother got, and Tara felt a swell of longing for their old home.

Sensing May's eyes on her, she tried her hardest to look happy as she ate. It didn't help that Kyle hadn't spoken a word since being called down for dinner. May continued to scrutinize her for a moment then rose to fill the kettle.

"Peter and I were just saying earlier how nice it is to have children in the home again. Family really is the most important thing in the world to us. We want you both to be happy here. Especially as we hope you'll be spending a lot more time with us from now on."

Her tone was light and happy, but the words dropped a veil of unease over Tara. Kyle seemed to sense the implication as well and frowned as he swallowed a mouthful of food.

Tara cleared her throat. "Maybe Mum can bring us here for holidays."

"Yes." May's long fingers folded together as she beamed at him. "Wouldn't that be lovely?"

A silence fell over them, but it wasn't the ordinary, comfortable kind. Tara hunted for something to break it with. "I was just thinking…I know almost nothing about you two. Do you work?"

May laughed as she fetched teacups and laid them out beside the boiling kettle. "Oh, goodness no, not for a long time. Peter's parents invested wisely and left him a tidy little nest egg, so we were able to retire early."

"What did you do before you retired?"

Peter and May exchanged a very brief glance, then Peter said, "May looked after the house. I did a bit of farm work."

"And, of course, we've always been very involved with the local community," May said. "Fetes, fundraisers, festivals…"

Tara put her cutlery back on her plate. "Did you have any other children? Mum didn't talk about siblings."

"Sadly no." The kettle clicked off, and May turned away as she poured the boiling water. "I would have loved more children, but life decided to withhold that blessing. Still—it worked out all right, didn't it? You're both delightful. I've never known such sweet children." She placed a cup beside Tara and stroked her hair again. "I know you must miss your mother dreadfully. But your grandfather Peter will take care of you. Now, would you like to play a game before bed?"

Tara's smile felt too tight. "Sure. But can I call the hospital first?"

"Of course, my dear. Of course."

Tara was very aware of May watching her as she went into the sitting room and dialed the rotary phone. She spoke to a new nurse who hadn't been on the ward for long and couldn't tell her much about Chris's condition—only that she hadn't woken. When Tara put the receiver down, May wrapped an arm around her shoulder in a soft hug and gently led her back to the dining room, where a new board game had been set up on the table.

She tried her hardest to be cheerful during the game. Kyle was no help; he'd withdrawn again, pulling into his own mind until it was a challenge to get even one-word answers out of him. Tara was relieved when the clock hit nine and May told them it was bedtime.

The house seemed to be creaking more than normal. Low, grating groans echoed around them as they climbed the stairs.

When Tara met Kyle in the bathroom, she saw spits of rain shining on the window.

"Looks like a storm," she said.

Kyle scowled as he scrubbed at his teeth with more aggression than they deserved.

"Kyle? You okay?"

He spat his toothpaste out. "Can I stay in your room again?"

"Yeah, of course you can."

Lightning arced across the sky, blinding them before fading. Kyle shook with the thunder, and Tara squeezed his shoulder to let him know it was okay.

They split up to change, and when Kyle arrived at Tara's room, he was carrying two books.

"What, not just one, but two?"

He glowered at her defensively. "In case I can't sleep."

"Don't think you're keeping the light on all night."

Kyle shuffled his bare feet over the floor, and Tara sighed. "Come on. Our fort's still set up. Grab a blanket and get warm."

Tara tried to nap for the following half hour while Kyle read, but the lamplight and the storm made sleep impossible. She finally rolled over and grumbled, "Aren't you ready for bed?"

"Not while it's storming." He sat with his back against the bed frame, the quilt draped over his head and his book propped up against his knees. Tara squinted at him, wondering if it was worth pushing to get the light off. It took her a few seconds to realize Kyle's eyes weren't moving. *He's still frightened.*

She looked toward the window. Rain lashed the glass, and

every flash of lightning highlighted the black forest. She chewed her lip, thinking. "What if we block the window?"

"You don't like your windows covered."

"I'll survive it for one night." Tara crawled out of their tent and went to the glass. Lightning flashed, and she saw two figures pacing over the lawn. Tara pressed her lips together and leaned forward, trying to see their faces, but as the lightning faded, the figures blended back into the inky darkness.

Is that Peter and May? What are they doing out in the storm?

"Is something wrong?"

She turned back to the fort. Kyle had poked his head through the gap in the quilt, his eyes huge in the lamp's dim light.

"Nah," she lied. "Just watching the rain."

Tara untied the curtains and pulled them together to cover the window. They were made from a thin, gauzy material that didn't do much to block the view. She sucked on the inside of her cheek as she thought then turned toward the wardrobe and eyeballed its width. "Hey, come and help me move this."

"Are we allowed?"

"I guess we should be. It's supposed to be my room now."

Kyle crawled out of the tent and took one side of the wardrobe. It didn't hold anything except a couple of Tara's shirts and jeans, so they scraped it across the floor without too much trouble. Once they'd lined it up in front of the window, they went to its front and shoved it against the glass.

A harsh cracking noise made Tara freeze. She looked down and swore. The base of the wardrobe had broken.

Kyle's face fell. "We're going to be in so much trouble."

"Shh, I might be able to fix it." Tara got on her hands and knees. One of the boards had come off, and she tried to push it back into place. It caught against something. She pulled the board back and looked behind it. A small black shape had fallen down to block the board, so she fished it out with two fingers.

"Cool, a book," Kyle said, and Tara had to muffle a laugh.

"Trust you to say that." She pushed on the board, felt it lock back into its slot, then picked up the book. It was narrow—barely a pamphlet—but the cover was leather. Dust and decades of grime had stuck to the surface, but when she wiped it clean, she couldn't see any title.

"Look on the first page." Kyle had crept up close to her, and his warm breath tickled her neck.

She grimaced against the sensation and opened the book to the title page. In dark-blue ink, "Christine's Journal—1985" was written across the page in flowing cursive.

Tara gasped and nudged Kyle. "Mum's diary. This used to be her room. She probably hid it in the wardrobe and forgot about it."

He jostled her back. "Then turn the page."

Tara did. The page was blank. She turned another, then another, and felt her heart sink as she realized the book was blank. "She never wrote in it."

"Jeez." Kyle slumped back as Tara reached the last page. "You'd think she'd at least have one entry. 'Dear Diary, I just got you this morning. I promise I'm going to write in you every single day.'

That's what I put in all of mine before forgetting about them forever."

Tara snickered and flipped back to the first page. A shadow by the spine caught her eye, and she opened the book. A series of ragged edges marked where pages had been torn out.

"Huh." Kyle bit his thumb. "Maybe she didn't forget about it, after all. Buy why'd she tear the pages out?"

Tara raised an eyebrow. "Unlike you, I *have* actually kept journals. And honestly, if there was even a tiny chance they'd be read, I'd burn them."

"Really? I'd think the whole blogging thing would harden you against that sort of stuff."

"Oh, don't worry, plenty of blog posts get deleted, too." Tara ran a finger along the ragged edges. "It's a shame she pulled them out. I'd like to know more about what she was like back then."

"How old would she have been?"

"Uh…" Tara counted back in her mind. "Sixteen or seventeen, I think."

"Shame," Kyle echoed. He kicked away from her and shuffled back into the fort, ostensibly to return to books that had words.

Tara sat cross-legged on the bedroom floor for a few more minutes, leafing through the paper and wishing her mother had left something of herself for her children to find. She'd joked with Kyle about destroying her own journals, but something about the situation struck her as unusual. *Why remove every page she'd written on but leave the book behind?*

Thunder crackled. The wardrobe did its job to mute the

noise and block out the light, so Tara opened the lowest drawer and put the journal inside. Suddenly feeling painfully, achingly lonely, she crept back inside the tent.

CHAPTER 9
UNLOCKED DOORS

HER FIRST THOUGHT WAS that her mother had come home early—but her mother had her own key; she never knocked. Maybe a neighbor needed something?

Tara crossed to the front door, passing Kyle stretched out on the couch and reading a book. Her fingers tingled as she reached for the handle. Her mind screamed at her not to open it, that bad things would happen if she did, that there was still time to avert the disaster, but her hand moved on its own.

"Tara Kendall?" The police officer's hair was bright red and curly and barely contained in a ponytail. She smiled, her teeth very white and dimples appearing in her cheeks, but the expression sent fear rushing into Tara's stomach.

"What happened?"

Her partner, a tall, flat-faced man, clasped his hands behind his back as he tilted his head toward her. "There's been an accident."

Tara twitched awake. Cold sweat drenched her and made her shiver. She felt behind herself, found the lamp, and turned it on.

Kyle slept on his side with his knees tucked under his chin. His breathing was slow and even, and Tara watched him as she waited for her pounding heart to slow. The storm had calmed, at least; she could hear rain beating against the house's side, but the thunder and lightning had stopped, and the wind no longer rattled the building.

Tap…tap…tap…

Tara crept to the quilt tent's opening and squinted at the door. A noise echoed from the other side, making her imagine fingernails being scraped against the surface. "May?"

The noise continued. Tara glanced at Kyle's sleeping form a final time then shimmied out of the tent. The night was cold, and she wrapped her arms around herself as her breath plumed from her lips.

Tap…tap…tap…

"May? Peter? Is that you?"

The tapping was accompanied by a soft shuffling. Tara hesitated then forced herself to walk toward the door. Her mind was filled with awful possibilities. The previous year, one of the blogger friends had written about his mother's stroke; she'd fallen in the bathroom, and mute and unable to walk, she could only knock on the door until someone heard.

Tara's mind constructed the image of May collapsed on the ground, her body twisted and her eyes locked open as she scrabbled at the door, silently pleading for help. Fear tasted bitter on her tongue, and she swallowed, reaching a hand forward. The air was still, almost suffocatingly close. Her lungs burned as she inhaled. She touched the cold metal handle, fastened her fingers around it, and turned it.

The tapping noise fell silent as the door gently swung open. Tara stared into the dim hallway but couldn't see anyone.

A low, grating groan made her gasp. The door next to hers—the locked door—drifted open, its hinges wailing in protest.

Fear clawed its way through Tara's body. Part of her wanted to wake Kyle so that she could have company, but she knew that would only make it worse. He would be terrified.

"May?" She whispered the words. "Peter? Is that you?"

No reply came from the open door. Tara could barely see inside from where she stood. Thin moonlight painted shimmers of light over some kind of furniture. She thought she saw a rocking chair. Was there someone sitting in it? She squinted and took a step closer.

The door slammed closed. Tara sucked in a gasp and pressed her hand over her mouth. The bang echoed through the old building; a thousand reverberations surrounded Tara before finally fading.

"Is something wrong, my dear?"

Tara turned. May stood at the top of the stairway. Her long gray hair hung in sheets around her shoulders, and her white nightdress appeared gray in the flickering light of her candle. Her face, normally so warm, was flat and filled with dark shadows. Tara's tongue was too dry to make noise. She mutely shook her head.

May didn't move for a moment, then a smile softened her expression. "You must have had a bad dream. Storms sometimes do that." She stepped forward, hand extended, and ushered Tara into her bedroom. "Go back to sleep, and try not to wake your brother."

"Okay." Tara's mind burned with questions. *What's in the room? Why did the door open? Why wasn't May sleeping?* But her head was still filled with echoes from the slamming door, and her tongue felt numb. She let May nudge her back into her room.

"Tara." May stopped in the doorway, her candle casting strange shadows over her face and brightening her eyes. "Stay in your room until morning. All right?"

She swallowed. "All right."

"Good night, my dear."

The door clicked closed, and Tara, certain she wouldn't be able to sleep, crept back into the tent. Kyle's eyebrows pulled together as he rolled over in his sleep. As Tara pulled a blanket around herself, she was grateful that she had Kyle to stop her from feeling alone.

CHAPTER 10
CLEANUP

TARA DOZED PATCHILY BUT woke before Kyle. Cooking sounds coming from downstairs told her May was awake, so she gathered clothes and changed in the bathroom. Thick fog had developed following the rain, and Tara couldn't see anything except white through the window.

A deeply stuck worry about what May might say about the locked room had dogged Tara through her dreams, but when she entered the kitchen, she was pulled into a brief hug before being shooed toward the table.

"Here," May said, her smile indulgent. "I cooked a special 'congratulations on surviving the storm' breakfast. I hope you like bacon."

Along with bacon were pancakes, fried eggs, fritters, and platters of fresh fruit. Tara's mouth watered. "Wow. Thanks."

Kyle appeared in the doorway, scratching at his messy, mousy hair and blinking in the light. Peter wasn't at the table, but as Tara sat down, she caught sight of him pacing through the mist at the front of the house.

May took her seat, smoothing her skirts down, and picked up her cup of tea. "Eat while it's warm, my dears. I'll bake a cake later. I think we need it today. You must have had uneasy sleeps—the storm passed right over us. It certainly kept me awake."

Tara glanced at Kyle. He seemed strangely subdued. Maybe he hadn't slept as well as she'd thought.

Peter passed the window again, his arm full of spindly branches and leaves. Tara tilted her head to the side as she watched. "What's Peter doing?"

"He's seeing what's broken and cleaning up a bit. Some trees came down last night."

Tara was feeling antsy, and the idea of burning some energy outside appealed much more than it would have if she'd had a computer. "Kyle and I can help. I don't really know about fixing stuff, but I can haul branches."

"Oh, you're sweet." May laughed. "I'm sure he'd love some company. Just don't overexert yourself. And finish your breakfast first."

"Sure." Tara shoveled food into her mouth, eating as quickly as she could without being rude, then nudged Kyle. "You ready?"

"Okay." He blinked twice, his green-gray eyes unusually serious.

Tara brought her plate to the sink then hesitated. "Um, but first—"

May gave an encouraging nod. "Yes, go and phone your mother, my dear. I hope she's feeling better today."

Tara hurried into the sitting room. As she lifted the receiver to her ear, she was met with a dull dial tone. She frowned, tried the hospital's number without success, and turned back to the kitchen. "The phone's not working."

"Perhaps a tree fell over the line. If that's the case, Peter will have a look at it."

She nodded then waited by the door for Kyle to zip up his jacket. As they stepped out of the house, tendrils of mist wrapped around them, and Tara blew out a wavering breath. "Icy."

"Yeah. Tara—"

Kyle broke off as Peter emerged through the fog, dragging a massive branch behind him. He nodded to them, and Tara matched his pace. "Can we help?"

"If you want. Pick up the branches around the house and pile them over there."

Dozens of felled tree limbs and fractured sticks littered the grass, and Tara filled her arms as she followed Peter toward the pile of debris he'd been building.

"I didn't realize the storm was so bad."

"Mm. We don't get them often, but they do a fair bit of damage when they come." He dropped his branch and turned back toward the house. "Not too much work this time. A few missing shingles and a cracked window. Could have been worse."

"Um…" Tara hurried to keep pace with him. "The phones seem to be out, as well. May said a line might have come down."

"That's exactly what happened. I'll see about having it fixed, but it'll likely be a few days."

Tara's heart plunged. Not being able to ask about her mother that morning was painful enough; she wasn't sure she could cope with days of radio silence.

Peter glanced at her and snorted. "Stop fretting, child. There's a pay phone in town. Ask May nicely enough, and I'm sure she'll take you." He bent to pick up a branch thicker than Tara's arm, slung it over his shoulder, and began dragging it to the pile. "She adores the two of you."

"She's been really kind," Tara said quickly. "You both have."

He grunted. Tara, not willing to let the conversation drop, gathered more debris as she kept pace with her grandfather. "I saw you and May outside during the storm last night. Did something happen?"

He sent her a quick glance then shrugged. "It's important to shutter the windows. Stop them from breaking."

"Oh." He was walking quickly, and Tara had to jog to keep up. "You should have woken Kyle and me. We could have helped."

His laughter was like a hacking bark. "No. May would have had a fit. It was too dangerous for kids."

Tara pursed her lips. "I'm fifteen."

"Still a kid," he insisted. "You don't get to be considered an adult until you can live on your own."

Kyle wanted us to stay by ourselves while Mum was in the hospital. We could have, too—probably would have, if Mrs. Jennings hadn't butted in. Tara knew the argument would have no power, so she swallowed it and dumped her branches on the pile. Peter straightened, pulled a cloth from his pocket, and used it to wipe mingling perspiration and condensation from his face. "Wish this mist would clear."

"Yeah." Tara frowned through the swirling white soup. She hadn't seen Kyle in several minutes. Faint unease niggled at her, and as Peter returned to hauling branches, she stepped into the fog.

The landscape was disorienting. When the mist swirled, trees and rocks blurred in and out of focus, creating the impression that they were moving. Tara squinted against the gray as she circled around the house, one hand brushing the stone corner as she passed it.

The vegetable garden was barely visible; only the tall, empty stakes identified it. They poked out of the earth like blackened matchsticks, and a figure paced among them.

Tara exhaled a held breath as she moved forward. "Kyle? What are you…"

The dark shape turned toward her, and Tara's words trailed off. It wasn't Kyle. The figure stood nearly a head taller than she was, despite its bowed shoulders. Long fingers twitched at its side as it tilted its head to regard her. Pit-black eyes, the only clear feature, shone in its sunken face.

A breeze moved the mist, making it swirl. A thick clump blocked out the figure, and when the mist cleared, the garden was empty.

Tara tried to make a noise, but fear squeezed her throat closed and made it painful to breathe. She staggered away from the empty lawn, frantically scanning the space for motion as her heart knocked against her ribs and her fingers turned numb. Her back hit something solid. She looked over her shoulder and saw she'd walked into one of the pine trees that grew around the house.

The wood was damp and held little patches of spiderwebs, but Tara dug her fingers into it, grateful for something solid and real in the realm of swirling mist.

That wasn't Peter. It wasn't May. It wasn't Kyle. Whatever it was, it can't be natural.

Memories of the smudged photograph resurfaced, and the shape behind Peter became much, much harder to explain.

Tara looked to her right. The house's corner wasn't far away, and beyond that, she would find the front door and the relative safety of indoors. She gave the garden a final, fearful scan then dashed for the porch.

Running through the mist felt worse than walking. The tendrils seemed to grab at her like invisible icy fingers. She skidded around the building's corner, her sneakers digging clumps of grass out of the wet ground, and nearly collided with a body.

Kyle, his arms full of branches, gaped at her as he staggered back. "What're you doing?"

"Kyle!" Relief drained Tara, and she bent forward, one hand pressed to her racing heart as she tried to reoxygenate her body. She couldn't speak for a moment, and when she did, the words came out harsher than she'd meant. "I was looking for you. Where *were* you?"

"Looking for *you*," he shot back. "I can't see anything in this mist."

Tara, still bent, shook her head. "I saw something. I don't know what. It was like a person. It turned to look at me, but then it just vanished."

"What? You mean it disappeared into the fog?"

"Yeah! It was there one second, then it disappeared."

Kyle dropped his armful of branches and shifted uncomfortably, his face screwing up as he scanned their surroundings. Tara had meant to warn him, not frighten him, but the end result was the same.

"It wasn't really clear." She forced herself to stand straight, despite the stitch digging at her side. "Maybe it was just a thick patch of fog. Or…or my eyes playing tricks on me."

His eyebrows were pulled low over his eyes. "I want to go back inside."

"Me, too. I hate this fog. Let's go."

As she turned, she felt a slight tug on her jacket. Kyle had taken hold of it. Tara mentally slapped herself; she hadn't meant to upset him. He'd seemed uneasy that morning, and talking about shapes appearing and vanishing in the mist wasn't going to help.

But maybe it's good for him to be wary of the mist. Her mind reconstructed the image: a man, tall but with bowed shoulders, standing among the freshly turned ground. The fog had blocked out everything except its silhouette. And then it had just…vanished. Tara tried to swallow, but her mouth was dry.

They found the porch's steps and moved into the relative safety of the house. Tara inhaled deeply once she was inside, glad to be out of the suffocating white.

"Tara? Kyle? Is that you?"

"Yes," Tara answered as May appeared in the kitchen's doorway.

She beamed at them. "I'm glad you came back inside. It's too hard to see out there—you could trip and break your necks. Instead, you can help me with my cake." She wiggled her eyebrows. "It's apple and walnut."

CHAPTER 11
WALNUT

KYLE LOOKED AS THOUGH he wanted to say something, but he clamped his mouth shut. He followed Tara into the kitchen, where May was bent over the oven. "Wash your hands, children, then start mixing the dry ingredients in the bowl. The recipe's on the bench."

Tara obediently scrubbed her hands in the sink, but her thoughts were worlds away from the mixing bowl and implements on the table. She looked through the window at Peter's faint outline as he dragged branches across the lawn. He bled in and out of the mist, and the sight made her shiver.

I have to ask. "May?"

"Hmm?" The woman's attention was on her task of greasing the cake pan, but Tara knew she was listening.

"Have you ever encountered something strange? Something you can't explain?"

May placed the pan down. It made a solid clunk on the wooden table, and for a moment, that was the only sound in the kitchen. Then she said, "What did you see?"

Tara licked her dry lips. She realized she was still scrubbing the tea towel over her hands, even though they were thoroughly dry, and forced herself to hold still. "I don't know. A man in the mist. I think. I don't know."

"Ah, I see." May smiled as she measured the flour. "Do you believe in ghosts?"

Tara didn't have an answer, so instead sent the question back. "Do *you*?"

May resealed the flour container. She set it aside and rested her palms on the countertop as she answered carefully. "There was a time when I didn't. But then I saw some things...things not unlike what you glimpsed yourself...and now, I...well, I suppose I try to keep an open mind."

"Oh," was all Tara managed to say.

Kyle glanced between them, his face pale and eyes huge. "Is this house haunted?"

"Goodness, you have such an imagination." May laughed and reached for the sugar. "I wouldn't go *that* far. If the dead linger, they certainly don't like to show themselves. I never saw anything conclusive—only hints and whispers."

Tara pulled up a seat and leaned on the table. "What do you mean by that? What things did you see?"

"A glimpse of motion in the forest. A sound that might have been either a bird or a girl calling my name." May measured out a teaspoon of nutmeg and dropped it into the mix. "Even if our ancestors do stay here, it's nothing to be alarmed by. I like to imagine they're watching over us and keeping us safe. Like guardian angels."

Kyle still looked unsettled, but less horrified than he had before. Tara was grateful. Unlike Peter, May had a soft touch and seemed to know how to calm Kyle.

Are ghosts real? That man in the fog—there one second and gone the next—there's no physical explanation for it. I can't imagine my eyes were playing tricks. Is that it, then? Definitive proof? And if so, is May right? Are they gentle guardians watching over us?

"Tara, would you bring me the milk from the fridge?" May waved a spoon at her. "All of this talk of ghosts is turning my helpers into distracted spectators."

"Oh, right." Tara ran to fetch the carton then made herself focus on the task at hand while Peter's silhouette continued to move past the window.

Once the cake was in the oven, May gave both Tara and Kyle a spoon each to lick then undid her apron. "I have a few little jobs to take care of. Will you two be able to amuse yourselves for an hour?"

"Definitely."

Kyle tugged on Tara's sleeve as he shot her a sideways glance. "I want to take a walk in the woods. Will you come with me?"

"You want to—in the woods?" Tara couldn't keep the surprise off her face. She'd never known her brother to willingly neglect a book in favor of nature. He scowled at her.

"I want to see where the paths go."

The fog had thinned, but Tara still didn't feel comfortable leaving the home. Kyle's stare was too insistent to ignore, though. "Well, uh, sure. It's okay, isn't it, May?"

"Stay within calling distance," she said. "And be back within the hour. The cake should be ready then."

Kyle tugged his jacket on then led the way outside. Tara hadn't seen him so enthusiastic about anything in a long time, and she had to jog to match his pace as they crossed the lawn. "What's gotten into you?"

"Shh," he hissed back. "I've been trying to talk to you alone all morning, you ditz. Didn't you get any of my hints?"

"Oy, don't be mean." She pulled a face. "And what hints?"

"I was winking!"

"Well, you might want to work on your technique. I didn't notice."

He grumbled something under his breath then stopped at the edge of the forest. They both turned back toward the house. The mist was thinning, but it still hung in tendrils across the ground. Peter was barely visible by the side of the building.

"What's the matter?" Tara asked.

"Just making sure we're not being followed. Come on." Kyle pulled his jacket up around his throat and hunched his shoulders as he stomped into the woods.

The atmosphere was wholly different compared to when they'd followed the trails with Peter. The area felt calmer and quieter—almost lonely. Tara stuffed her hands into her pockets and shivered when drops of water hit her neck and trickled under her jacket. Kyle's behavior was starting to unnerve her. "Okay, we're far enough away. They won't hear us. What happened?"

Kyle sent a final glance down the path behind them then slowed his pace to a shuffle. "I had a dream last night. I guess it was really more of a nightmare. Do you remember how when we were younger, we stayed with one of Mum's work friends?"

"Uh…vaguely." Tara pursed her lips. "Her name was Sue, wasn't it? We spent like three weeks there."

"Do you remember *why* we visited?"

"Be…cause…she was a friend?"

Kyle scowled at her, and Tara huffed out a breath. "Well, obviously *you* remember, so quit playing twenty questions and just tell me."

"I'm just…" He dug his fingers into his hair. The frustration twisting his face made Tara feel guilty for being so flippant. "I'm trying to separate memories from imagination. I've got to know I'm not making this up."

Tara squeezed his shoulder. "Okay. Take it slow. Tell me what you remember, and I'll tell you if I can remember it, too."

"It happened ages ago." He closed his eyes and tilted his head toward the canopy. "Sometimes at night, I'd hear a noise outside my window. I'd sit up and look outside and see a man standing there, staring up at me. I'd scream and wake Mum up, but when she looked, the man was gone. She'd tell me it was just a dream."

"Yeah, I remember that. You'd cry when she tried to put you to bed because you were afraid the man would be there."

"And…" He couldn't make eye contact. "*Was* it a dream?"

Tara tried to think back. She remembered it happening not long after Kyle started school, which meant she would have been ten and Kyle six. They'd shared a room, and four nights in a row, Kyle's screams had woken her. "Probably. Mum made you return a bunch of books to the library because she thought one of them was causing it."

"You never saw anything?"

Tara shook her head. The window had been on Kyle's side of the room, but when she'd looked through, she'd seen only the narrow alley running beside their second-floor apartment. "You said he stood under our window, in the streetlamp light. But it always happened around midnight. You must have been asleep."

"I used to read under the covers."

"You still do—and fall asleep with your flashlight left on. Where's this going?"

"I'd forgotten about it until last night. I had a dream about it. More of a nightmare, I guess. It was so vivid, and I could see the man's face clearly. It looked a lot like Peter's."

Tara stopped walking. "You're saying the phantom man under your window was Peter?"

"I-I don't—" He flapped his arms, frustrated. "I don't *know*. That's why I'm trying to find out what you recall. When we first met Peter, I thought his face looked familiar. But am I remembering something that actually happened? Or was the man outside my window just a dream?"

"It's got to be a dream, surely."

Kyle turned his wide, helpless eyes toward her, begging for

some form of confirmation. "I saw the man four days in a row. And then, on the last day, Mum took us to visit her friend Sue. You remember that, don't you?"

"Yes…" Memories rushed back to Tara, and they spread uneasiness through her insides like cold cement. She remembered being shaken awake by her mother. *Did I forget to tell you? I promised to visit Sue this weekend. Come on, grab some clean clothes. We need to go now.* Tara licked her lips. "We drove three hours in the middle of the night. I was so irritable; we barely even knew Sue. And she didn't have a room ready for us or anything."

Kyle was nodding, watching Tara intently. "And we stayed there for *ages*. For no reason. And Mum kept making phone calls late at night and would get angry if I tried to listen in on them."

The path took a bend and began trending downhill. Tara followed it without paying attention to where she was stepping. "What are you thinking? That the man was *real*? That Mum saw him one night and…and we fled?"

"It didn't seem strange at the time. But we missed three weeks of school. And we stayed with someone we barely knew, even though her place was smaller than ours."

Tara rubbed at the back of her neck. "She only let us live with her for three weeks, but then we moved to a new apartment not much later. Do you remember? It was the one above the Chinese shop. We only stayed there for, like, six months before moving to where we live now."

"He looked like Peter," Kyle said, his tone decisive. "Same face shape. Same eyes."

Fear and frustration were crowding Tara's brain. She rubbed her hands over her face and took a slow breath as she tried to think. One part of her said, *You're the responsible one. Don't get carried away with conspiracy theories.* The other half said, *If this is true, it's really, really bad.* She struggled to find a rational middle ground. "Are you sure you saw Peter's face? Or was that just how the man looked in last night's dream?"

Kyle shrugged. "Kinda sure. Not totally."

They followed another bend in the path. Tara knew they were starting to drift too far from the house, but she wasn't ready to turn around.

"There's something else." Kyle flicked his eyes toward her then averted them.

"Okay. I'm listening."

"How did May and Peter know we needed somewhere to stay?"

"What do you mean?"

"Well, if they had no contact with Mum, how did they know about her accident? Did Mrs. Jennings call them, or did they call the hospital, or…what?"

Tara bit her lip. "There's probably a database or something. Next-of-kin contact details. The hospital would have phoned them, and somehow, they got in touch with Mrs. Jennings."

"Mum never spoke about them. She never called them. Never visited. They may as well have not existed. Would the hospital really have their contact details on her record?"

"I don't know." Tara tried not to let frustration into her voice. "What's the alternative?"

"Dunno. It's just weird." He scowled at his sneakers. "All of this is weird. *You're* the one who phones the hospital to ask how Mum's doing. They haven't checked on her even once. It's like they don't care about her. And they keep talking like we're going to spend a lot of time here, when everyone at the hospital was saying it would only be a few days."

Queasiness threaded through Tara's stomach. She folded her arms over her chest and breathed through her nose. "This probably doesn't mean anything. It's…it's a bunch of coincidences layered on top of each other. There's no way May and Peter *want* Mum to be hurt. She's their *daughter*."

Kyle shrugged but kept his gaze on the ground. "Let's go back. I don't want to get in trouble for being out too long."

They'd wandered farther than Tara had intended. The trees grew thick and high above them, blotting out the natural light and making the day feel five degrees colder. Patches of oddly colored mushrooms grew around the stumps, and lichen drooped off the boughs in heavy shawls. Tara shivered and turned. "Yeah. Let's go."

They took two steps, then Kyle pulled up short. Tara turned back to him, hoping he didn't have another revelation to cram into her already-full brain, but he wasn't looking at her. His owlish eyes were fixed on the space behind her as color bled out of his cheeks. "Graves."

"What?" Tara followed his gaze to a shadowed hollow inside a cluster of pines. Two slate-gray tombstones poked out of the dark earth.

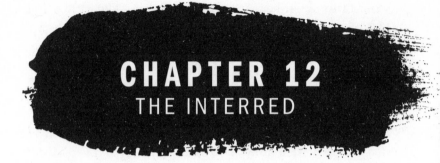

CHAPTER 12
THE INTERRED

"NO WAY." TARA STEPPED closer to the graves and tried to read their names in the dim light.

"Tara?" Panic bled into Kyle's voice. He hung back, and Tara waved to him.

"Just stay there a moment. I want to know who they are."

The stones were rough and worn. Unlike the markers she'd seen in cemeteries, they looked hand-chiseled. She knelt to get closer and squinted as she read the uneven words in the stone. "Petra…1975. George, 1975. They don't have surnames."

"*Tara*, you're on the graves."

"Oh." She scooted backward. A slight slope was all that remained to show where the graves lay. Weedy grass and a lily-shaped vine covered the dirt. "I wonder who they were. May and Peter would have to know about them, right? This is part of their property, and they've lived here since before the seventies."

"I want to go home." Kyle's voice was a tight whine. Tara turned and frowned.

"You're not scared, are you? They're just graves."

"Graves belong in *cemeteries*, not in *homes*."

He sounded close to crying. Tara rose, dusted dirt off her jeans, then put an arm around Kyle's shoulders. "Sorry. Let's go back to the house."

Kyle gradually calmed as they followed the winding path back to the house, but he was still sniffling as they stepped into the clearing. "C'mon," Tara said and squeezed his shoulders. "Everything's okay. You know that, right? You've got me with you. I won't let anything bad happen."

"Yeah," he mumbled, but she felt him shake as they neared the building. Tara tried to keep her voice bright and her face clear, but the walk had left her feeling jangled. She couldn't stop replaying the conversation. *If Kyle really saw Peter below his window when he was a child, what does that mean? He was only six. Is his memory even accurate?*

May met them on the porch and cooed when she saw Kyle's blotchy face. "What happened, my dear? You didn't hurt yourself, did you?"

Kyle didn't answer, so Tara shrugged. "We found, uh, some graves, I guess. It startled Kyle."

"Oh!" May's eyes widened a fraction, then a warm smile covered the surprise as she wrapped an arm around Kyle's shoulders. He stiffened but didn't try to pull away as May led him into the house. "You poor thing. That must have been a shock. Sit down—the cake's just cooling, but you can have a slice with ice cream. That should help."

Tara inhaled as she followed them into the house. The kitchen smelled amazing. She slid into the chair beside Kyle, who'd fixed his eyes on the white cloth. Tara bumped his foot under the table. *Don't be rude.* His scowl intensified.

"Here we are." May put generous pieces of the cake into bowls and began scooping the ice cream. "I didn't expect you to get so far from the house. You found your great-grandparents, my dears. Petra and George Folcroft—Peter's parents."

"Why did you bury them here?" Tara asked. "Why not in a cemetery?"

"A few reasons." May handed out the plates then took her seat opposite Tara. She'd only given herself a small cube of the cake on the side of her teacup. "The town was much smaller at that time—there were really only a handful of families settled there—and the graveyard was very lonely and not a welcoming place. Peter and I discussed it and decided Petra and George would have been happiest staying near the house they'd built and on the land they loved." She shrugged. "The Folcrofts have always been a close family. It didn't feel right to relegate them to some stranger's land where they were never visited. This way, we can keep them close and never forget them."

Kyle shivered, but Tara couldn't tell if it was because of the graves or the ice cream he was shoveling into his mouth.

Tara folded her arms on the tabletop. "Were they nice people?"

"Oh, the nicest. Even though I'd only married into the family, they made me feel like I was their daughter. George loved to garden. He spent hours in the patch behind the house every day. He grew the biggest pumpkins I've ever seen. And Petra had such a big heart. I still have some of the clothes she knitted and the tablecloths she crocheted. I wish you could have known them."

Tara glanced at Kyle to make sure he was okay with the conversation. As far as she could tell, he'd tuned them out to focus on his cake. "Did Mum know them?"

"Very briefly, though she wouldn't remember it. She wasn't quite two when they passed away."

Tara remembered that the year of death—1975—was only a year after her mother's birthday. She licked her lips. "Tell me about Mum. What was she like when she was growing up?"

"Oh!" May laughed and clasped her hands below her chin. "She was such a fiery child. Always thought she knew best, and always getting into trouble. I was heartbroken when she left… but children can't stay children forever, can they? Peter and I always knew she'd move through life like a shooting star, burning so brightly that people would stop and watch."

Tara examined May's face as she talked. Her eyes sparkled, and her cheeks glowed with emotion. Part of the uneasiness that had grown that morning subsided. *Kyle was wrong. May still loves her daughter. She still misses her.*

"When she's better, I hope we can all come back to visit," Tara said.

"Yes." May's voice took on a dreamy quality. "The whole family together again. I would like that very much."

The front door creaked, then Peter appeared in the entryway, looking tired as he stretched. May bounced up to put the kettle on and slice him some of the cake. "How are you faring out there?"

"Good and bad." He grunted as he took his seat and scratched through his steel-gray hair. "The house is safe, but there are trees down blocking the driveway. I'll get the chainsaw out this afternoon, but it'll take a few hours to clear the path. Should be done by tomorrow, then you can take the kids to use the pay phone."

"What a good idea," May said. "Will you be all right waiting until then, my dears?"

"Yes," Tara said then hesitated. "Or maybe we can try our cell phones?"

"They won't work," Peter said. "No signal. But I'll clear the road as quickly as I can."

Tara glanced at Kyle, who still wouldn't look up from his bowl. "I really appreciate that. Thanks."

The afternoon passed slowly. Tara offered to help Peter with removing the fallen trees, but May refused to let her be around the chainsaw. The night of missed sleep eventually caught up to her, and she napped inside the quilt tent while Kyle steadily processed the collection of books. Her dreams were fragmented and disquieting, and more than once, she pictured herself standing at the window of their old apartment and staring down at a shadowed man lurking in the alley below.

May served pasta and meatballs for dinner. Tara chatted with her grandparents through the meal and happily answered their questions about her school and her friends then delved into an explanation of how blogs worked. May listened, enthralled, and called her remarkably clever, but Tara was fairly sure she still didn't understand the concept. Neither Peter nor May seemed interested in technology beyond radios and cars.

Kyle was silent and sullen through dinner. When they finally met in the bathroom to brush their teeth, she said, "What's up with you?"

"They're lying." He spoke around a mouthful of frothing toothpaste. "They don't really miss Mum. They're just saying what they think we want to hear."

"That's ridiculous." Tara rinsed her toothbrush, dropped it back into the cup, then folded her arms. "You know what I think? The new house and new routine are hard to get used to. You're absorbing all of that anxiety and turning it into paranoia. Now you've built a bad dream and a couple of offhanded words into this crazy conspiracy theory. May and Peter have been nothing but generous and kind, and you're refusing to even talk to them. It's rude."

"Fine." He slammed the tap off. His lip was quivering, which was always a bad sign. "You can have your stupid fort to yourself. I'll stay in my own room tonight."

"Now you're being petulant."

He sent her an intense, furious glare then stalked out of the bathroom. Tara twitched as the door slammed, then rubbed a hand over her face.

I'm not wrong, am I?

CHAPTER 13
CHARCOAL

TARA GLOWERED AT THE floor as she made her way back to her room. *I'm doing a garbage job of looking after Kyle. He needs his real mother. She'd know what to say to make him relax.*

She tried to picture her mother's face. The memory was blurry, and some of the details felt off. Shock squeezed at Tara's heart. *I can't be forgetting what she looks like; it's only been four days.*

As she scrambled to pull back all of the details that made up her mother—chestnut hair, eyebrows that pulled up when she smiled, wide lips counterbalanced by a long nose, the tattoo ringed around her upper arm—another more recent image resurfaced. The familiar face swollen and mottled as it lay on the hospital whites. Tara grimaced. She wanted to cry, but sound traveled in the house, so she clenched her teeth to keep herself quiet as she entered her room.

Her tent had been dismantled. The chair and bedside table

that had held the quilt up were pushed to opposite sides of the room, and the wardrobe no longer blocked the window. The furniture hadn't been moved back to its usual place, but shoved away haphazardly as though in anger. Mouth open, Tara stared at the scene. Her first thought was Kyle—but she'd heard him go to his room after their fight. *Did May do this, then? Or Peter?*

Tara picked up the limp quilt then let it drop back onto the floor. The idea of a blanket fort suddenly seemed childish and stupid. Maybe that was why her grandparents had dismantled it—as a message that it wasn't acceptable behavior.

More tears prickled at her eyes. She scrunched her face up to keep them inside as she lifted the mattress back onto the bed and returned the dresser to its correct place. The wardrobe was too heavy for her to move herself, but on impulse, she opened it and retrieved the journal from the floor.

She and Kyle had only had a couple of minutes to pack before leaving for their grandparents'. They'd brought clothes, toiletries, and books, but neither had thought to bring anything that belonged to Chris. The journal was the closest thing Tara had. She placed it on the bed next to her, curled into a ball, and stared at the leather cover as she tried to remember only the nicest memories she had of her mother.

Sleep took a long time to come, and when it did, it was filled with more uneasy dreams. She was running through a forest as a man with a rifle stalked her. Just as she thought she'd escaped, she looked down and saw she was racing along a dock. Water trapped her on three sides, and the man came out of the woods behind, rifle raised. Tara pulled to a halt at the end of the dock and saw a girl's face staring out of the water, her mouth open as she begged to be released from her grave.

Tara jolted awake. She felt sick and bent over her lifted knees as she waited for her stomach to quiet and her heart to slow. The clock on her bedside table said it was nearly one in the morning. Moonlight glossed over a white shape, and Tara saw the journal lay open beside her. *Did I open it in my sleep? Or did it fall open with my tossing?*

She picked it up with sweaty fingers. The row of torn page stubs created a jagged shadow running down the journal's center. Moonlight landed on the paper—what would have been the next page for an entry—and Tara's eyebrows pulled up. The sheet had tiny, faint shadows over it, almost like words.

The pen must have indented the page below the one it was writing on. Excitement built inside Tara. She carefully rotated the book as she tried to make out the imprinted words. It was impossible—the lines were too faint to make out letters. She threw off her bed sheets, wrapped her dressing gown over her pajamas, then took the book and stepped into the hallway.

If I can find a pencil or some charcoal, I might be able to make a rubbing of it. She looked toward Kyle's room. A faint light under his door told her he'd fallen asleep with his lamp on. Guilt hit her, but she swallowed and turned toward the staircase. *I shouldn't have snapped at him. He's scared and confused, and he needs an ally. I don't want to wake him, but I'll apologize tomorrow.*

Tara hung to the stairs' outer edge to minimize the creaks, but they were still noisy enough to make her grimace. She stepped into the hallway and pressed her lips together as she considered her options.

She still hadn't seen the entire house. A study or workroom would probably have normal pencils, but Tara needed something softer that would leave graphite on a page without crushing the indents. She doubted either May or Peter owned soft art pencils—there weren't any artworks hung on the walls—but she decided to look for some, anyway.

Tara tried the first door she came across, which led to a tidy laundry. Beyond that was a dining room with a table long enough to seat eight. The area was clearly long untouched, suggesting May and Peter preferred to eat in the more cheery kitchen.

The third, fourth, and fifth doors were all locked. She couldn't guess why so much of the building had been barricaded, but it made her feel uneasy. The final door she tried let her into a lounge area. Overstuffed armchairs were grouped around a fireplace, but like the dining room, it seemed to be a part of the house that wasn't visited often. The fireplace was a good sign, though, and Tara hurried to kneel in front of it.

The hearth had been cleaned since its last use, but a layer of soot coated the internal stone wall. Tara opened her mother's journal, tore a page out of the back, and laid it on top of the sheet that held the precious indents. Then, moving as slowly and as carefully as she could, she scooped some of the soot off the wall and brushed her fingers over the page.

A creak made her startle and smudge some of her work.

Mouthing furious words, Tara twisted to look behind her. The room was empty. The doorway was a black cave, hiding countless tangled shadows, but she couldn't see any movement in them. *It must have been the wind.*

She turned back to the paper. The rubbing wasn't clear, but to Tara's delight, patchy words had started to appear. She continued moving her fingers until she'd gone over the entire page then held it up as she tried to read it.

Two words appeared to her immediately: *lies* and *parents*. Tara worked to piece together the broken patches of light and dark around them. Her mother's teenage scrawl was only faintly reminiscent of her neat adult writing. The words seemed to run off the lines in some places. Tara wondered if that was how Chris normally wrote or whether it was a result of heightened emotions. From what she could glean from the entry, Chris had been furious when she wrote it.

"They finally admitted…lies…all these years my…parents…" Tara tilted the page, trying to get more moonlight on it. There was a gap in the words, then a phrase written near the base of the page. "…to leave. Anywhere is better than here. The ghosts… restless."

Tara tried to quiet her buzzing mind. *Chris must have seen ghosts at the house, too.* Was it possible they were more prevalent than May had implied?

A soft exhale made Tara swivel. A woman stood in the doorway. Her white nightdress swirled in a nonexistent wind, and her hands hung limply by her sides.

Tara collapsed backward, her heart thundering, and pressed her hand across her mouth. The woman stood frozen in the entryway for a beat then stepped into the room, her glassy eyes focused on one of the windows. Moonlight fell across her face, and Tara sucked in a quick breath. "May?"

May didn't respond to her name but continued walking toward the window. She passed so close that Tara could have reached out and touched her flowing nightdress. Her face was slack, her eyes wide and unfocused, and her breathing slow.

She's sleepwalking. Tara staggered to her feet, the journal and charcoal page clutched to her chest, and backed away from the older woman. May stopped at the window and pressed her fingertips to the glass. "Mother…"

The word, so quiet that Tara almost didn't catch it, left a patch of condensation on the glass. Tara kept shifting away as she reached one hand behind her to feel for the doorway. Icy-cold fingers brushed hers, and Tara gave a choked cry as she turned. The space behind her was empty. May continued to stare through the window, but Tara was certain she could feel eyes fixed on her, watching her, following every motion.

She turned and ran for the stairs. Not caring about staying quiet anymore, she dashed up the steps two at a time, her heart thundering in her throat and fear making her skin prickle. She passed her own room and continued to Kyle's, only catching herself as she skidded to a halt beside the door.

"Kyle?" She kept her voice to a whisper as she tapped on the wood. Someone moved inside, then the door opened.

Kyle, his face pale, blinked up at her. "Couldn't you sleep, either?"

She shook her head. He stepped back so that she could enter his room, and she saw he still had his mounds of books stacked across the neatly made bed.

"I'm sorry," she said as soon as she had her tongue under control. "I shouldn't have snapped at you."

He shrugged awkwardly. "You were right. I was being rude. I just…I…"

Tara squeezed his shoulder to let him know she understood. "It's all right. We're going to be all right. Yeah?"

"Yeah."

CHAPTER 14
PHOTOGRAPHY

SUNLIGHT FELL OVER TARA'S face and pulled her out of sleep. She rolled over and saw Kyle was still curled into a ball, his arms wrapped around his pillow. It was early morning, and the night animals' cries had given way to bird chatter.

Tara lay still as she processed the previous night. May had frightened her, but the more important knowledge had come from the charcoal copy of the last page from her mother's journal. She guessed Chris had left the home shortly after writing it. She'd been seventeen at the time. The falling out must have been big to make her think she'd be better off on her own.

They finally admitted…lies… Tara turned to glance at Kyle. He thought their grandparents were lying, too.

She wished she could speak to her mother. Did she regret the rift that had grown between her and her parents, or was she grateful for it? Was there a reason why Tara had never met May and Peter before?

She forced herself to get up and go to the bathroom to wash and change. She could hear May cooking breakfast downstairs, but she wanted space to think more than anything. When she was presentable, Tara returned to her own room and leaned on the windowsill as she watched the yard below.

The rattle of an engine told her a car was coming. Peter's Jeep emerged from the driveway, circled to the front of the house, and parked. He must have been clearing the road, as promised. Tara hoped she could convince May to take them to the town early. She had two days of news to catch up on. Fear and hope churned in her stomach.

She'd left her camera on the bedside table. Tara examined the two Polaroids she'd left under it. Now that she'd seen her mother had written about ghosts in the journal, Tara found herself assigning more significance to the blur behind Peter. *What if this house really is haunted—and not just in a whispers-and-glimpses sort of way, but actually significantly haunted? They'd have to be the ghosts of Peter's parents. Is May right—are they really watching over us? Are they trying to communicate? Or do they want something more?*

Remembering the icy fingers that had grazed her hand the night before, she reflexively clenched her fist. The camera still had film in it. Tara bit her lip, picked it up, and jogged downstairs.

"Good morning, May! Can I take a walk before breakfast?"

"Of course, my dear." May looked worlds away from the slack-jawed figure that had walked through the house the night before. She wore her familiar apron over a floral-print dress and had pinned her hair up. "Breakfast will be ready in twenty minutes, all right?"

"Thank you!" Tara jogged down the porch then swiveled, trying to think of the best place to take her pictures. She had limited film and didn't want to waste it.

The vegetable garden again. May said George Folcroft had loved gardening; he might haunt there.

Faint mist created an ethereal glow over the area, though it was nowhere near as bad as it had been the day before. Tara stopped beside the recently planted ground, aimed her camera to capture as much of the area as possible, and took her picture. She then paced backward until she was nearly at the trees and took another photograph of the house. With both pictures developing in her pocket, she chewed over her options of what else to capture.

What about the gravestones?

She turned to face the woods, equal parts uncertain and excited. Dew clung to the leaves and weedy grass spaced between the tree, and some kind of bird warbled farther away.

I should have time. It's not that far—it was a shorter walk than to the lake. I'll be quick.

She hung the camera's strap around her neck and paced around the clearing's edge until she found the pathway she and Kyle had taken the day before. Bird chatter surrounded her as she followed the twisting dirt path deeper into the woods. When she thought she was close, Tara had to slow down and scour the side of the trail to make sure she didn't miss the grave markers.

They waited in the little hollow between pine trees, and she stopped to examine the two rough rocks with names chiseled into the front. Tara, worried she might not be alone, bowed her head respectfully before stepping back and focusing her camera. She got as much of the area in her frame as possible then took the picture. The black square whirred out of the camera, and she tucked it into her pocket.

It's weird. May talked about loving family so much and burying Peter's parents on the property to keep them close, but these gravestones look like they haven't been visited in a decade.

Weedy grass grew over the graves, and lichen clung to the rocks. The trail had an aura of neglect, too—nature was gradually encroaching over the path.

Underbrush crackled behind her. Tara squinted into the woods, searching for motion. *Just a bird.* She repeated the phrase to herself as though saying it enough would make it true. "Just a bird, just a bird."

The noise was too loud for any bird she'd ever seen, though. Something heavy was moving toward her, crushing leaves under its feet and snapping branches. Tara clutched her camera close to her chest, wishing she'd brought Peter's gun. A splash of blue moved between the trees, then a familiar figure stepped onto the path.

"Kyle?" Tara pressed a hand to her thundering heart as tension bled out of her. "What are you doing here?"

He still wore his pajamas. His hair was tangled and his eyes unfocused as he shambled toward Tara, then past her, continuing down the path.

"Kyle?" She jogged after him. "Kyle, you're scaring me. Say something."

His face was emotionless, the muscles all slack. It reminded Tara horribly of how May had looked when sleepwalking the night before. Fear flooded her mouth with a sickening metallic tang, and she grabbed Kyle's shoulder to stop him. He twitched, then his eyes widened. He blinked first at Tara then at the forest, as shock and confusion transformed his face. "What...? Where are we?"

"In the forest." Tara tried to swallow, but her mouth was too dry. "You were walking around like a zombie. What happened?"

"I..." He turned in a semicircle, stared at his surroundings, then looked down at his pajamas in horror. "I don't know. I needed to go to the lake."

"Were you sleepwalking?"

"I don't know!" His voice grew tighter and higher.

Tara exhaled and pulled Kyle into a quick hug before turning him in the right direction. "C'mon. Careful where you step. There's probably thorns around here and everything."

They walked slowly. By the time they stepped back into the clearing, the mist had vanished and the sun had started to warm the crisp air. May must have seen them from the kitchen window, because she ran out of the house as they neared it. "Kyle, what are you doing out in your pajamas? And no shoes! Are your feet hurt?"

He shrugged and mumbled an incoherent excuse.

May sighed deeply and cupped his cheek. "Be more careful,

dear. I'd be heartbroken if you were hurt. Now quick, go upstairs and change for breakfast. I'll keep yours warm for you."

Tara started on her food while Kyle jogged up the stairs. May fussed about the kitchen, and Peter sipped his coffee. Neither was paying attention to Tara, so she pulled the photos out of her pocket.

The picture of the gravestones showed nothing she hadn't seen with her own eyes. She set it aside, thinking it would make a great addition to the blog saga she was constructing in her mind. The second picture showed the garden. At first, Tara was disheartened that it was empty, too, then she saw the smudge at the edge of the photo.

It had barely been captured, but she was sure she could make out a man's shoulder and half of his face. She held it inches from her nose as she tried to make out more details. She saw a collar, a shadow that might have been whiskers, and an orb of light where his eyes should have been.

Tara tried to keep her breathing steady as she set the picture aside. The final photo showed the house. It looked strange in the Polaroid's warped colors, as though it had come out of a different world. It took Tara a moment to find the anomaly. A woman stood in one of the upstairs bedrooms, her silhouette visible behind the curtains.

Ghosts. Tara's heart thundered. She peeked at May and Peter, wondering if she should say something.

Kyle came thudding down the stairs. He skidded into the kitchen and took his seat at Tara's side. She nudged the photos toward him and indicated to the relevant places. His face scrunched up, and for a second, Tara thought that maybe she shouldn't have shown him. Then he whispered, "Ask them."

"Here we are." May set a plate before Kyle and nudged the fork toward him. "You must be hungry after tramping all through the woods."

"May?" Tara waited for the older woman to settle into her seat then pushed the photographs toward her. "We want to talk about the ghosts."

CHAPTER 15
SPECTERS

TARA LAID OUT THE photographs in a neat line before May. The woman glanced over them and smiled. "I'm so glad to see you like the camera."

"Look here." Tara pointed to the smudges and the white-clad figure in the window. "Do you see them?"

May's expression was perfectly serene as she met Tara's eyes. "Yes, my dear."

"Well…what are they?"

"What do you think they are?"

Tara was quiet for a moment, and May's smile twitched wider. Tara licked her lips and glanced at Kyle, who nodded for her to continue. "They're ghosts."

"You're right, darling." May lifted her cup and sipped the tea.

May's calmness was unnerving. Tara squeezed her hands

into fists below the table. "Yesterday, you made it sound like there *might* be ghosts. But now you're talking like you've known all along."

May drew a deep breath and let it out slowly as she looked toward the ceiling. For a moment, Tara could hear only the quiet ticking clock in the hallway and a cricket outside the window. Then May said, "One of the hardest parts about welcoming you into our home was knowing how much to tell you. Peter and I talked it over for hours. We wanted you to know the truth…but on the other hand, you were—are—only children."

Tara tightened her fists. The palms were sweaty, but she kept her face neutral as she watched her grandmother. She didn't need to look at him to know that Peter was examining her over the top of his coffee mug.

"In the end, we decided on a compromise. If you were curious enough to uncover it on your own, we'd be open about it. If not, we wouldn't say anything." May smiled. "You're both so clever. I'm glad you found out. I didn't like keeping secrets."

"So…so…" Tara struggled to find the right words. "There are ghosts here. And you see them…a lot?"

"Not too often. Perhaps every couple of days. More often, if you're looking for them."

"Oh." She turned to Kyle. His eyes were huge and his face pale, but the set to his lip told her he wanted answers just as much as she did. "How many are there?"

"A few. Your great-grandma and great-grandpa. Peter's sister and brother."

Peter shifted forward. "I told you I go to the lake sometimes to talk to Anna. I don't often see her, but I can feel her."

"This is insane," Kyle muttered. He dragged his fingers through his hair. "Why can we see them? I've never heard people talk about ghosts like this before. I've never *seen* a ghost before."

"Oh, poor dear." May reached out to touch him, but Kyle shied away. She sighed and leaned back in her chair. "Truthfully, I don't know why they linger here. We have always cared deeply about family; perhaps they didn't want to leave us after death? It might be something in the ground. It might be something in the family genes. I couldn't tell you."

Tara squeezed her hands together. "And you're just…happy to let it happen? Haven't you thought about calling a priest or something?"

May laughed. "Of course not. They're friendly, Tara. They're not like the ghosts in scary campfire stories. They watch over us. It's a comfort—it helps us to not feel as alone."

A thought occurred, and Tara frowned. "When we saw people walking outside the house at night… The man who was all bent and the people during the storm…"

"Those were your great-grandparents, yes. Forgive us for lying. We only wanted to protect you." She tilted her head to the side, her eyes crinkling with a fond smile. "If you find things in your room moved, they're usually responsible for that, too. They like to help like that."

We're living in a haunted house. Tara looked down at her lap, where she still squeezed her hands together to keep them from shaking. May kept promising the spirits were friendly, but Tara couldn't feel easy. She imagined the ghosts watching her as she slept, and horror made a shiver course up her spine.

It's normal for May and Peter. They've lived like this for decades— they don't see anything wrong with it.

She looked toward Kyle and saw her same worry reflected back in his eyes. It was easy to say "don't be afraid." Following that advice was impossible.

"If I'm not mistaken, I think Peter might have finished clearing the driveway," May said.

Peter released a gruff laugh. "Yes. We're no longer trapped, thank goodness."

"In that case, now might be a good time to go into town." May stood and picked up their plates. Tara hadn't eaten much, but she didn't object—her appetite was thoroughly gone.

She knew May and Peter had deliberately changed the subject, but she didn't mind. The promise of access to a phone and a chance to get away from the house's heavy atmosphere were tantalizing. Tara was glad to drop the topic of ghosts for the short term.

The siblings retrieved their jackets then waited by the door as May put on her hat and took the key ring off the metal hook by the kitchen. Kyle brought an armful of books with him. Tara ended up holding onto a stack of them so that they didn't fall off the seat when the Jeep went over ruts and bumps. When May asked why he'd brought them, he said he wanted to return them to the library.

"Aren't they any good?" May asked.

"No, they were fine. I've finished them, that's all."

Tara stared at him then scoffed. "I don't believe that. Some of these are huge! How did you get through them?"

He sent her a sly glance. "By turning the pages."

"Smart aleck."

May only laughed. She seemed in a good mood. Tara wished she could feel the same way as she leaned against her window and watched the trees flash by.

Ghosts. They're real. I've seen them. It was still hard to believe. Her mind instantly went to how she would structure a blog series about it—but she knew her friends would think she was either joking or trying to prank them.

Maybe this is why Mum left. She hated seeing the spirits everywhere.

The trees were replaced by small houses and stores as May turned into the town. She found a parking space in front of the greengrocer's and stepped out of the car. "The pay phone's just up here," she said as she took her purse out of her bag and shook out a handful of coins. "Do you remember the number?"

"Yes, thank you so much." Tara took the coins and jogged toward the bright-red pay phone tucked off the side of the street. She held the receiver between her shoulder and ear as she dialed the number then started feeding coins into the slot. They dropped straight into the return tray.

She frowned. *Am I doing something wrong?* There weren't any instructions posted. She tried pressing on the hook then put another coin into the slot. It fell straight back out.

"Phone doesn't work," someone shouted, and Tara jumped. She turned to see a plump man poking his head out of the barbershop next to her. He shrugged. "Broke this morning. Bad timing after the storm and all—a lot of people have been trying to use it."

"Oh." Tara hung up the receiver, feeling the anticipation that fluttered in her stomach shrivel into stress. "Is someone going to fix it?"

"Hell if I know. They probably will if enough people complain." He shrugged again. "Sorry."

Tara collected the coins and turned back to the Jeep. May waited with Kyle at her side. The crushed look on Kyle's face told her they'd heard the barber.

"I'm sorry, my dear," May said as she took the coins back. "We'll get our home phone reconnected as soon as possible."

"Thanks." Tara knew her smile wasn't quite natural but didn't know how to fix it.

"Would you like to use the computer? We can stay in town for a while if you like. We could even have lunch here."

"I'd like that."

May beamed as she led them to the library. She waited while Kyle passed his books over the counter then said, "If you need me, I'll be in the greengrocer's. Otherwise, I'll come back in an hour."

"See you then."

They split up—May back onto the main street, Kyle into the shelves to search for books he hadn't yet read, and Tara toward the back of the building, where the ancient computer promised an hour of escape from her reality.

The machine hadn't been turned on that morning, and she had to wait while it booted up. As she watched the loading screen's circle rotate for what felt like an eternity, she realized she wasn't excited. Normally, she craved getting on the computer first thing every morning and again when she got home from school; it was like an itch that wouldn't go away until it was scratched. As the internet browser opened and she began typing in the URL, she found she didn't really care about reading her comments or seeing what her friends had posted. For the first time since she'd started it, her blog felt hollow.

This better not be what growing up feels like, because it sucks. She logged into her account. The post she'd made the last time they were at town was short, and it had only four replies—three wishing her good luck and one asking for an update. She created a new post and titled it Stuff's Getting Weird.

Super-quick update. I'm pretty sure my grandparents are keeping secrets. The room next to mine is locked, and they won't tell me why. I found my Mum's old journal, and it talks about ghosts. My brother's freaking out, which is freaking me out. If I mysteriously go missing, please know that you're all my BFFs and I want my comic collection donated to alexis.the.great. Peace.

The last part had been intended as a joke, but it felt too close to home. Tara pulled a face as she pressed the publish button. She leaned back in her chair and began scrolling through the updates that had been posted since she'd last been on. There were a lot of them, but they weren't grabbing her interest like they normally did.

I wonder if I could call the hospital from this computer? Tara searched the installed programs for Skype but didn't find it. Based on the browser speed, downloading it would take more than the hour she had. Even if she could get it installed, the call quality would be abysmal.

She looked up the hospital's website. They had their phone numbers listed, but no public e-mail address or contact form. Tara chewed on her lip.

A thought had been growing since Kyle had shared his theory the day before. Tara felt ridiculous for even considering it, but the niggling curiosity refused to go away. She gave the unappealing blog posts a final glance then opened the browser history.

It hadn't been cleared in a long time. Someone had searched for how pay phones worked the day before. *They probably encountered the broken machine down the street.* Tara found the links to her blogs from two days previously. She kept scrolling back, passing cooking archives, Wikipedia links, and an assortment of inappropriate sites from someone who didn't know how to use private browsing. Even farther back were searches for how big plesiosaurs grew, cat flu symptoms, the age of the world's oldest man—someone settling a bet, Tara suspected—and a site about car mechanics.

Tara stopped scrolling. The car site had been visited ten days before, just a couple of days prior to their mother's accident. The user had reached it by searching "how car brake lines work."

"Tara Kendall?"

She looked between the two police officers as fear made her stomach flip. "What happened?"

"There's been an accident," the taller one said.

The officer with the curly red hair and the too-bright teeth reached out to touch Tara's shoulder. She was speaking, but the words sounded jumbled. Accident. Car's brakes failed. In the hospital.

Tara tasted a bitter, metallic liquid, telling her she'd bitten her lip too hard. A ringing noise filled her ears. She turned toward the shelves where Kyle sifted through the volumes. She opened her mouth to call him but then closed it again.

Don't get carried away. What did you tell Kyle last night? A series of coincidences can make a person paranoid.

She looked back at the search results. "How car brake lines work." She scrolled back up to the top of the list. The search result from the day before read "how pay phones work." The barber said the phones had broken that morning. Tara had watched Peter's car pull into their property that morning. She'd assumed he'd been clearing the driveway, but he would have had plenty of time to take a trip into town before the stores opened.

Tara stood. Dizziness made her stumble, and she grabbed at the computer's desk. She closed her eyes while the sensation passed, then she turned toward the library's door. Neither Kyle nor the librarian paid any attention as she left.

CHAPTER 16
BREAD AND MYTHS

SHE HESITATED ON THE sidewalk and blinked against the sun. The morning felt calm, and she was alone on the street, save for an elderly lady coming out of the drugstore and a car coasting down the street. The greengrocer's was to her left. She turned in the opposite direction. It didn't take long to find the bakery's sign swinging from its awning.

The door's bell jingled as she entered. The store's small café portion took up the front of the store, and a display case of decorated cakes and fresh bread stretched down one wall. The café was empty. Pattie, the lady who'd interrupted Tara's blogging, leaned on the counter as she chatted with a younger assistant. Pattie looked toward the door, and her eyebrows rose as she saw Tara. She said something to the assistant then came around the counter. "I wasn't expecting to see you here. Everything okay?"

"Sure," Tara lied. She rubbed a hand over the back of her neck. "Um, do you have a moment to talk?"

Pattie smiled, but the expression held a grim undertone. "Definitely. Do you want something? A drink? Cake?"

"Water would be great. I don't have long."

Pattie nodded to an empty table then disappeared into the back of the store. She came back with two cups of water and a plate of cookies and set them on the table as she sat. "It's Tara, isn't it?"

"That's right."

"And you're staying with May and Peter with your brother?"

"Kyle, yeah."

Pattie whistled. "You'll have to forgive my surprise. After all this time, I was starting to think you were fictional."

Tara shifted forward. "What do you mean, 'after all this time'?"

"Well, May's been talking about you for years. Her dear grandson and granddaughter. 'He likes reading; she's a photographer. They're going to visit us soon.' It was always soon—they'll come and stay with us soon; you'll get to meet them soon—but you never materialized. Most people wrote it off as the regular Folcroft weirdness." Pattie squinted at Tara. "You're not in any kind of trouble, are you? I don't mean to pry, but…"

"It's fine. I…I'd rather not talk about it right now." Tara took a sip from her glass to wet her tongue and calm the rushing in her head. "When you said regular Folcroft weirdness, what are you talking about?"

Pattie made an uncomfortable murmuring noise. "I don't mean to be rude. I'm sure they're lovely people and good grandparents."

"Please, tell me."

The baker's shoulders slumped as she exhaled. "All right. Well, the Folcrofts have been living in their little nook in the mountains for as long as anyone remembers. The late Folcrofts were some of the founding members of the town, but May and Peter have almost nothing to do with us anymore. They don't have any friends. No one knows much of anything about them, except they rarely leave their home and they have two grandchildren who were coming to visit one day."

"May said you don't like her because she beat you in a baking competition."

Pattie barked a laugh. "I'd like to see her try! No, she's never joined any competitions. Or attended town meetings. Or come for the town parties. They drive in on Mondays to do their shopping, make a few minutes of small talk, then disappear for another week."

Tara chewed on her thumb as she tried to reconcile this knowledge with her impression of her grandparents. "Did you know my mum at all?"

"Christine? Poor thing. We were around the same age, but I didn't know her. She was hardly ever allowed in town, and when she was, she came supervised. I heard she ran away when she was seventeen. I wish she'd come to me—I would have tried to help her." Pattie frowned. "Is she doing okay?"

"Yeah." *Except for the coma…* "She's a legal secretary. People like her."

"Good. I'm glad to hear it. She deserves a nice life." Pattie pursed her lips. "Sorry, I'm talking out of turn again. I guess if she let you come visit, she must have mended things with her parents."

"What else do you know about the Folcrofts?" Tara asked.

"Uh…not much. I mean, there's a whole pile of myths about them. But most probably aren't true."

"Tell me."

She snorted, looking equal parts amused and uncomfortable. "You're keen. All right. Supposedly, the late Mr. Folcroft came into a lot of money during the war. The rumor says that he made his fortune as a spy…for the other side. He sold state secrets in exchange for a small fortune. When the war ended, he went to ground, hiding in that mountain house that no one can find unless they know where to look. Some people say he was only a spy for the money. Others say he never dropped his allegiances and continued to harbor fugitives even decades after the war."

"Did you ever hear anything about…" Tara's tongue refused to form the word *ghosts*. She swallowed and tightened her grip on the glass of water.

"Tara, please tell me if this is out of line, but are you in some kind of trouble? Do you need help?"

Yes. No. I don't know.

Pattie's eyebrows were so high, they were nearly hidden under her frizzy bangs. She looked on the verge of saying something else, but then the bell jingled as the door slammed open. A sickening wave of dread washed over Tara before she even heard the voice.

"Tara. Come here."

May stood in the doorway, her face blanched and her eyes unexpectedly cold. Tara didn't dare hesitate but rose and crossed toward her grandmother as fear pounded through her veins. May scanned Tara's face then shot a glare at Pattie. Taking hold of Tara's shoulder, May pulled her onto the street.

I screwed up. Tara tried to swallow, but her throat was too tight. Kyle waited on the sidewalk, his terrified eyes focused on the asphalt. He flinched as the bakery door slammed closed. May's eyes flicked between the siblings as she took a slow breath, then she said, "Get in the car."

Kyle shot his sister a sideways look, silently asking for guidance. She gave a tiny nod, and together, they walked back to the Jeep.

May waited until their seat belts were buckled before climbing in the driver's seat. A soft click told Tara the doors had been locked. Then the engine revved, and the car screeched out of the parking space and back toward the mountain.

She's furious. Tara dug her fingers into the car's seats. *I crossed a line. What's going to happen to us?*

May had only ever smiled and cooed at them before. This new, stony-faced, cold-eyed creature was foreign and frightening. Tara, desperate to mitigate the damage, cleared her throat. "Grandma May—"

"I hope you don't mind leaving early." Her tone was upbeat, but it didn't match her expression. "It looked like rain, and I remembered I had washing on the line."

The sky was clear, and Tara was certain the washing line had been empty when she'd taken her photos that morning. She glanced at Kyle then tried again. "I'm sorry, Grandma."

"Whatever for, dear?" May finally smiled, but the expression didn't look right. "You're old enough to explore the town on your own." Somehow, the natural act was more unsettling than the anger.

"Anyway," May continued as she turned into their driveway. "We probably won't be going back for a little while. It will do us good to spend some time as a family. Just the four of us. You'd like that, wouldn't you?"

"Yes," Tara and Kyle chorused as the trees closed in to block out the sunlight.

CHAPTER 17
BUNKER

"BE CAREFUL," TARA SAID.

She and Kyle strolled across the open patch of ground in front of the house. Whenever Tara looked behind them, she saw May watching through the kitchen window.

Kyle had his hands forced into his pockets. His walk would have looked relaxed except for the stiffness in his shoulders. "What happened? Why were you in the bakery?"

"I was trying to separate imagination from fact. A bit like you with your dreams." Tara pretended to kick a rock. She hoped, from May's perspective, it would look like a casual stroll before lunch, not a rushed meeting. "You were right, by the way. Something strange is going on."

"I'll save the gloating for later. Tell me what you know."

She looked at him. His glare was defiant. *He deserves to have the truth.* "I don't think Mum's crash was accidental. Someone looked up info on car brakes a few days before her car failed. And I think Peter tampered with the pay phone, too."

Kyle made a noise that sounded somewhere between a sob and a laugh. "You're lucky I'm already miles down the rabbit hole; otherwise, I'd call you crazy."

"I know. And it's still possible this is all a coincidence. Right now, all I have is circumstantial evidence. Nothing concrete. No proof. But Pattie says the Folcrofts have always been weird loners."

"To be fair, both you and I could be classified as weird loners, too."

"True."

"But at least you have the internet as an excuse. May and Peter live up here with no computer, no TV, no jobs, hardly any books…not much of anything, really. Don't they get lonely or bored?"

Tara shrugged.

"So what do you think happened?" Kyle asked. "Be honest. What's the worst-case scenario?"

"Worst case…May and Peter are crazy, control-obsessed sociopaths. They wanted grandchildren. They stalked our family for years. When they couldn't kidnap us, they tried to kill Mum. And here we are."

Kyle blew out a breath. His shoulders were shaking.

"Best case," Tara continued, "all of this is a really bizarre series of misunderstandings and coincidences. Maybe Pattie *does* have a vendetta against May. Perhaps someone unrelated wanted to look up how to repair his car brakes. Maybe the accident really was an accident."

"If fiction has taught me anything, nothing's a coincidence."

Tara shrugged. "In their defense, May and Peter haven't done anything bad to us. They've been the textbook definition of perfect grandparents."

"That we've seen."

"Yeah." Tara thought back to the presents on their first day at the house: a book and a camera. The gifts matched hobbies they'd both held five years previously—around the same time Kyle had seen the man below his window. "I'm not sure how many coincidences I can believe in, either."

They were nearing the forest edge but had to turn away from the trail that promised privacy. May had said she didn't want them wandering off so close to lunch.

Kyle rubbed his fingers through his hair, his forehead creasing with a frustrated frown. "Do we have a plan? Is there anything we can do?"

"I'll try to get our mobiles back when May and Peter aren't looking. But I don't know how easy that will be; May seems to spend most of her life in the kitchen. In the meantime, we stick together and look out for each other, okay?"

"Yeah. We'll keep sharing a room. Don't let them separate us."

Tara gave him a tight, frightened smile. "And act like everything's normal. If the worst-case scenario is our reality...I feel like things will only be happy as long as they think they have their perfect family."

"Children! Lunch!"

They turned toward May, who stood in the house's doorway and waved to them.

"Okay," Kyle said. He snagged Tara's jacket hem. She let him hold on as they returned to their new home.

Lunch was unpleasantly quiet. May made an offhanded comment about the weather being nice. Tara quickly agreed. Peter grunted. And the following fifteen minutes were spent in silence.

Kyle kept his eyes on his plate. He ate quickly and pushed away from the table as soon as he was done.

"Stay," May said, extending a hand. Tara tried to read her expression, but she gave nothing away. "I want to show you something in a minute."

Kyle hesitated then sank back into his chair.

May took her time finishing her meal. By the time she took their plates to the sink, Tara's stomach was knotted into anxiety. She'd loved surprises before coming to the Folcroft house. But, despite their calm delivery, May's words created a slow, steady undercurrent of dread.

"We're going outside." May stacked the dishes then undid her apron and hung it on the pantry door's hook.

Peter looked up from his mug. "May."

She gazed at him, and Tara had the impression that a silent conversation was taking place.

After a moment, Peter grunted and shrugged. "All right."

"Come on, children." May took the key ring off the hook by

the door then passed Tara and Kyle their coats. "It's not far, but better that you don't get chilled."

Kyle kept silent as they stepped into the yard, but his fists were clenched so tightly that the knuckles stood out white. Tara gave his wrist a quick squeeze. *I'm here. We're in this together.*

May led them toward the woods, in the opposite direction of the lake. Her strides were long and smooth, and she didn't look back to check whether her grandchildren were following. As they neared the edge of the clearing, Tara realized they were heading for the concrete structure she'd noticed when she first arrived.

They stepped through the copse of trees sheltering it, and she was able to see its form clearly. The concrete wedge rose out of the ground, its highest tip reaching slightly above Tara's head, and a metallic door was fixed into the slant facing the house.

May sifted through the ring then fitted one of the older, rustier keys into the door's lock. The key screeched as it turned, and the door shuddered as its hinges tried to stick. May pushed the door wide open to reveal a staircase leading into the ground.

"Inside, children." The placid voice held no menace, but it terrified Tara. Kyle's shaking fingers found her hand, and she squeezed back. She stared at the black opening, her heart fluttering unpleasantly and her throat squeezing tightly.

May tilted her head to the side and raised her eyebrows. "Is something wrong? You don't need to be afraid of the dark. There's a light inside."

Will she be angry if we refuse to go in? Tara licked her lips. Kyle's hand was sweaty and held hers too tightly. May watched, eyebrows held up, head tilted toward the door expectantly. *There's nowhere else for us to stay. We don't have a choice except to do what she wants.*

Tara stepped into the stairwell. Cold air rolled out of it, engulfing her and making her shiver. Kyle followed closely, his breathing quick and shallow.

"Don't be frightened," Tara whispered, and the hushed phrase bounced off the walls squeezing around them.

The stairs were too narrow for more than single file. As Tara peered over her shoulder, she saw May following them. That offered a small measure of relief. At least they weren't being locked inside.

"Keep going." May's voice echoed, making it seem like a dozen of her were speaking. "The floor evens out soon."

The farther they went, the less natural light accompanied them. Tara had to reach out a hand to feel the walls. They were dry but cold and rough—either stone or concrete.

She stumbled as the stairs turned into a passageway. With Kyle and May blocking the retreat, her only option was to move forward blindly. She took a dozen steps before her shins banged into something solid. Tara grunted and bit her tongue.

"Sorry, my dear. I should have warned you." With a click, a single bulb came on above their heads. Tara blinked at her surroundings.

They were in a small, narrow concrete room. The ceiling ended just above her head, and the space was barely long enough for the three of them to stand. Tara looked down and saw she'd walked into a wooden chair. The seat, the light, and three empty shelves on the back wall were the only furnishings.

"This is our bunker," May said. She stood, blocking the escape, with her hands pressed against the walls. "Peter's parents built it during the war. They had to construct it quickly, which is why it's quite small."

Kyle's voice was quiet but clearly audible in the still air. "Why are you showing us?"

"They made a mistake when they built it." May closed her eyes and inhaled. "They made it airtight to keep toxic fumes out but forgot to install any kind of ventilation. And because it's so small, a person can only stay in here for a few hours before suffocating."

Tara's heart beat so loudly that she was sure the others must hear it.

"The door closes easily and needs the house keys to unlock. If you became trapped in here, you probably wouldn't be found in time." May's long fingers caressed the heavy metal door that divided the stairwell from the room. She smiled.

She's going to lock us in. Tara's fear swelled into panic. She felt for Kyle's hand and squeezed his trembling fingers. *Get ready to run.*

"You're curious children." May exhaled, and her hands dropped off the walls. "I realized this morning that I've let you explore all around our house but haven't warned you about the bunker's risk. What would I do if I lost you? How could I survive if you were hurt because of my negligence?" She looked at Tara, and the awful placid expression had been replaced with real human concern. "I'm showing you this so that you know not to play in it. No matter how tempting cubbyholes are, this one is too dangerous. All right?"

"All right," Tara croaked.

May turned back to the stairs. "You're good children. Let's go back indoors. I'll bake you some sugar cookies."

CHAPTER 18
EYES IN THE DARK

TARA SAT UP IN bed with her knees tucked under her chin. Kyle slept, but his face kept twisting as dreams disturbed his rest. The alarm clock read just after two in the morning. She'd been listening for close to forty minutes, but the only noises were the animal screams echoing from the woods and the creak of old wood shifting in the breeze.

This is my best chance. She slipped her feet over the edge of the bed. It was a cold night, and her hairs rose as she went to the door and looked out.

The hallway was empty. Moonlight flooded through the window at one end, its glow lighting up the wooden floor. Tara crossed to the stairs then eased her way down them as slowly and carefully as she could. The boards groaned. Tara clenched her teeth with each creak, but when she reached the landing, the rest of the house remained quiet.

The kitchen looked strangely surreal at night. The curtains were drained of their pastel color as they fluttered in the wind. The furniture sent long shadows stretching up the walls, and the ticking clock in the hallway sounded unnaturally loud.

Tara went to the sink and reached for the wicker basket hidden on the shelf above. It was heavy, but when she pulled it down, she found it was full of spoons. Frowning, she sifted through the cutlery then worried at her lip as she tucked the basket back on its shelf. *May moved the phones. But where?*

Tara turned in a circle then began opening drawers as quietly as she could. The kitchen impressed her with how carefully it had been arranged; all of the cupboards and drawers were packed immaculately. None held the missing phones.

A floorboard creaked above her head, and Tara froze. She held her breath as she waited for the noise to repeat, then, when it didn't, she slunk into the hallway.

If I were May, where would I hide the phones?

She ran her hands through her hair, afraid that the answer might be something she would never think of, then chose to start in the family room. She searched around the dusty bookshelves, through the desk's drawers, and even around the couch cushions.

Another floorboard creaked. Tara straightened, her heart thundering. The noise had come from the direction of the stairs. Had she woken May or Peter, after all?

Tara began creeping backward. Another board groaned, this time, in the hallway. Tara, her breath shallow, reached the curtains beside the window. She pressed into the space behind them, hoping the poor light would help make her invisible.

Shuffling footsteps moved through the hallway. They reached the room's open door and paused. Tara squeezed her eyes closed, her pulse thundering so loudly that she was sure the figure in the doorway would hear it. Then the footsteps continued down the hallway. The door creaked as it opened. Then, a second later, it clicked shut again.

Tara pulled air into her starving lungs. She felt dizzy from stress but didn't dare move from her hiding place. She turned her head to look through the window in case the person came around the house's corner.

They didn't, but motion drew her eyes to the big tree near the front of the house. The old, weather-worn swing moved in long, slow arcs. Tara's heart froze as she glimpsed the outline of a small boy sitting in it, his legs moving in time with the swing as moonlight flashed off his eyes. Tara blinked. The swing was empty, but it continued to move in the wind.

Tara crept out from the shelter of the curtains. As valuable as the phones were, she only wanted to return to the security of her room. She crept to the hallway and back up the stairs, keeping her feet light, and drew a relieved breath as she gently nudged the bedroom door open.

The bed was empty. Tara's relief crashed into dread. She rounded the bed in case Kyle had fallen into the stack of books beside it, but there was no sign of him. Premonition drew her to the window.

A small, lone figure crossed the lawn. Moonlight shone off Kyle's mousy hair as his shadow, unnaturally long, wavered behind him.

Tara muttered quick, furious words under her breath as she pulled her shoes out from under the bed and tugged them on. *He must be sleepwalking. We made a promise to stick together. I shouldn't have left him.*

She stopped in the hallway and faced May's room. Half of her mind said she needed to wake her grandmother. The other half insisted it would be safer if it was just her and Kyle. She squeezed her lips together and turned away without making a noise.

There wasn't time to be overcautious on the stairs. Tara could only try to stick to the edges and grimace at the noise. She reached the hallway and raced for the door.

Cold air hit her as she stepped outside. She took only a second to cushion the door's swing so that it wouldn't slam then turned and began running across the lawn.

The swing continued to move in slow, steady arcs. Now that she was outside, she could hear the noise; the rope created a low, hoarse creak as it shifted against the ancient branch. Tara gave it a wide berth.

Kyle had already disappeared into the forest. Multiple paths led into the woods in that section of the clearing, and Tara hadn't seen which one he'd taken. She flexed her fingers as she glanced between them, hoping one might give her a hint about which direction her brother had gone.

This morning, he walked into the woods while sleepwalking. He said he was going toward the lake. She took a guess at the correct direction and plunged into the forest.

The light was too poor to make out anything except vague shapes. Tara had to squint at the ground to make out the worn path and any protruding tree roots or hollows. Unlike the trail leading to the gravestones, the path to the lake seemed worn and compacted with use.

A branch crunched to her right. Tara froze and peered through the trees. She couldn't see Kyle's blue pajamas. She kept moving.

Branches snagged at her clothes and scratched her exposed arms and face. Every few meters, the canopy cleared enough for patches of light to dapple the forest floor. Insects hummed around her, and a bat screamed as it burst out of a hollow trunk. Tara risked wetting her lips. "Kyle?"

The silence was damning. She quickened her pace, eyes fixed on the ground and hands outstretched to protect her face from branches. Cold sweat coated her, sticking her pajamas to her skin and racking shivers down her back.

Another branch cracked behind her. Fear thrummed through Tara, with harsh doubt following in its wake. What if Kyle wasn't following a path? When he woke, he wouldn't know which direction to follow to get home. How many days could he wander the forest without water? One? Two?

"Kyle!" Her voice was raspy and cracked. "Kyle, answer me!"

Leaves rustled. She thought she heard an exhale, but when she turned, she was alone. Tara squeezed her hands into fists and willed her eyes to stay dry. She increased her pace to a jog.

The trees thinned. Shimmering water stretched ahead of her. It looked almost magical, like a sheet of diamonds undulating in the wind. The only dark shape was the pier stretching over the water…and the small figure walking toward its end.

"Kyle!" Tara broke into a run. She was breathless and shaking, but she forced her legs to move faster and faster as she raced Kyle to the end of the pier. He moved as though he were dazed, rocking with each step and unresponsive to his name. He reached the end of the pier and continued walking, one foot extending over the inky, diamond-speckled water. Tara's fingers snagged the back of his pajama top, and she wrenched him back.

They both hit the wooden dock. Tara, winded, kept her grip on Kyle as she tried to catch her breath.

"Wha—" Kyle's eyes widened as he blinked up at the night sky. Panic infused his voice. "Where are we? How… What…"

"Sleepwalking," Tara gasped then gave his shoulder a soft punch. "You jerk. You gave me a heart attack."

He sat up, his tousled hair falling in his eyes. He looked at the water then at the forest behind them and wrapped his arms around himself as he shivered. "How'd I even remember the way here?"

"Beats me. You're welcome, by the way." Tara rubbed her hands over her face. Her heart beat so quickly, it hurt, and her hands were shaking. But being released from fear's grip was almost euphoric. She reached up and patted Kyle's shoulder as he continued to stare around them. "We should go back to the house."

"Yeah."

For a moment, neither of them moved. Tara looked up at the stars. There were so many compared to the city's skyline. It was almost a mirror of the sparkling water below them. The lake lapped at the pier's supports, making a gentle slapping noise against the wood. A cold wind raced over her skin. She shivered and finally stood. "C'mon. I'm freezing."

Kyle still didn't budge. His round eyes stared over the water, and Tara thought he'd fallen back into the trance. Then she saw what he was fixated on, and her heart skipped a beat.

A girl floated under the water. Her dark hair spread out behind her like a halo, her arms spread wide, her head turned toward the sky. Her pale nightdress seemed to trail behind her for meters before fading into the water.

Kyle's hand found Tara's arm and squeezed hard enough to hurt. She stared at the figure floating so peacefully. Then the girl turned her head toward them, and her eyes, stained black, fixed on them.

"Go," Tara hissed, tugging Kyle with her as she backed off the pier. "Go, go, quickly."

Anna, Peter's drowned sister, opened her mouth as though she wanted to speak, but only two tiny bubbles drifted out. She began to drift upward, her body moving closer and closer to the lake's surface.

Tara and Kyle reached solid ground, and Tara pushed her brother toward the pathway leading into the woods. She kept her attention fixed on the water as she followed, afraid to look away but equally afraid of seeing more. As she reached the forest's edge, she caught sight of a hand stretching over the edge of the pier and landing on the wood. The drowned girl dragged herself up the structure, water pouring from her as she fixed hopeless black eyes on Tara.

Then the trees hid Anna from sight. Tara was grateful. She didn't want to see how far the girl would follow. She kept one hand holding onto Kyle's sleeve and the other reached ahead of her as they raced through the woods. Their ragged breathing and the crash of undergrowth being crushed were all she could hear for several minutes. Then Kyle slowed and eventually came to a stop, doubled over and gasping.

"Stitch," he managed between breaths.

"Okay." Tara leaned against a tree, winded and shaking. "Man, we are so unfit."

He laughed, but his eyes were shining with tears. "Are we far from home?"

"Dunno." She scanned the trees but didn't recognize any of them. "Probably not far."

An owl called from somewhere behind them, and its mournful note hung in the air. Kyle straightened, took a deep breath, and nodded. "I'm ready. Let's go."

A twig cracked behind them. Tara turned, skipping her eyes over the shadowed trunks and the darkness between them. She swallowed and nudged Kyle toward the path. *It's nothing. Don't let it freak you out.*

"Hey," Kyle whispered. "Did you see that?"

"What?"

"Something moved over there."

Tara followed his pointing finger. There was something between the trees; dappled moonlight hit its shoulder as she shifted. Tara's heart flipped unpleasantly. She followed the shoulder toward a broad, tan face, flattened ears, and two huge, amber eyes.

The mountain lion held her gaze for a split-second then slunk forward, ghosting between the trees like a silent phantom. It was massive. Tara had always imagined cougars were only a bit bigger than a wolf—but the beast dwarfed her. The twitching whiskers were longer than her hand. White teeth glistened as its lips pulled back. Its wide eyes, bright and eager, focused on Tara. The paws were as large as her head. And with each step forward, it moved a little faster, first walking, then trotting. Finally, it broke onto the path at a gallop.

Tara reacted on instinct. She leaped back and raised her hands to protect her face. Her feet bumped into a tree root and pulled her balance away. She hit the ground. The round golden eyes never left her as the cougar, as silent and sleek as the night wind, leaped.

Kyle shrieked. Tara felt the paws hit her chest, their weight phenomenal, but then they bounced away. Motion blurred in front of her, then Kyle stood between her and the cougar. He swung a branch at the beast like a sword.

"Get out of here!" Kyle's screams were raucous from fear. "Stupid cat! Go, go!"

The cougar froze, its ears perked as it assessed the boy. It took a step forward. Kyle didn't back off. Instead, he charged the cougar, swatting the branch at it, bellowing an incoherent yell. The cat's ears pressed onto its head, and it moved two paces back, tail twitching frantically. Again, it hesitated.

"Go!" Kyle yelled.

A hissing rumble reverberated out of the cougar's chest. Then it turned and vanished back into the woods, its movements as smooth and silent as they had been during the approach.

Kyle held his stance for a second, feet braced and branch held high. Then he sagged and turned back toward Tara. His face was ashen.

She pressed a hand over her mouth as she stared at the boy in front of her. Kyle the coward. Kyle, who never seemed to leave his fantasy worlds. Kyle, who still needed a night-light and cried during thunderstorms. He'd charged a cat that was at least three times his size…and won.

Terrified tears shone on his cheeks as he let the branch drop. His mouth twitched into a wobbly smile, then he held out his arms and ran to Tara. The hug was tight enough to force the air from her lungs.

"Okay?" he mumbled. "You okay?"

"Yeah." She hugged him back, shivering and nauseous, laughing with relief. "That was amazing. And stupid. But mostly amazing."

He laughed too, but it held a note of hysteria. Tara held him close, unwilling to let go. She only pulled back when the sound of crashing footsteps made their way through the shock. A familiar voice yelled, "Children!"

Tara turned to Kyle. "They heard us."

CHAPTER 19
JUSTIFICATION

PETER REACHED THEM FIRST. The loose pants and shirt were obviously his pajamas, but their casualness was undermined by the rifle cradled in the nook of his arm. When he saw them, he slowed to a halt and scanned the forest. "Either of you hurt?"

"No," Tara said, but May's frantic cry drowned out her answer. The older woman dropped to her knees and pulled them both into a hug.

"My children," she gasped, running shaking fingers over Tara's hair. "Please, please not my sweet children."

Tara frowned. "We're okay. Everything's fine. It was a cougar, but Kyle chased it off."

May leaned back far enough to examine their faces, and Tara was shocked to see tears running down her wrinkled cheeks. Warm hands cupped Tara's face then ran over Kyle's hair. "Thank mercy." She smiled, but the expression was shaky. "You terrified me. I thought…I—"

Peter stalked back to stand at her side and squeezed her shoulder. He was breathing heavily, but his expression was placid. "Best get them back to the house, May."

"Yes." Relief chased the fear out of her voice. "Back inside, where it's safe. I'll make you something warm to drink. My poor darlings."

She held their hands as they followed Peter down the path. He kept his rifle cocked over one arm, his head sweeping from side to side as he watched for motion. If the cougar was lingering nearby, it didn't show itself.

Tara was still shaking. She kept sneaking glances at Kyle. While he obediently held his grandmother's hand, his face had an odd expression. He didn't meet her looks.

May let them go once they were inside the house. She ushered them into the kitchen while Peter left his rifle beside the front door and disappeared up the stairs.

"We'll make it nice and cozy," May said as she pulled a saucepan out of a cabinet and poured milk into it. "Peter's gone to put the heater on. You two must be freezing."

Tara *was* cold, but she didn't answer. May hurried around the room, her long white nightdress and gray hair flowing behind her as she turned on lights and heated the milk. Peter returned, carrying thick quilts and slippers. He dropped the slippers by Kyle, whose feet were still bare, and May wrapped the blankets around Tara's and Kyle's shoulders.

"Coffee," he grunted to May.

"It will be ready in a minute."

Tara tried to catch Kyle's attention, but his eyes were fixed on the table as a frown creased his forehead.

Peter took his place at the head of the table and rubbed his hands over his face. He blew out a groaning breath. "What the hell were you two doing outside?"

"Don't scold them," May said pleasantly and tapped his shoulder as she moved past. "They're safe, and that's all that matters."

Peter continued to frown, so Tara cleared her throat. "Kyle was sleepwalking."

He grunted, clearly not happy, and leaned back in the chair.

"Don't mind Peter." May put two steaming mugs of hot chocolate on the table. "He can sound abrupt when he's frightened. He's not actually angry."

Tara nodded and pulled her cup close to her chest. May had added two large white marshmallows; the bobbing lumps were starting to melt. It looked a lot like the hot chocolate their mother made when it rained. Her throat tightened.

"I'm glad you're safe." May eased herself into the chair opposite. Her eyes were still glassy, but color had returned to her face. "I don't know what I would do if either of you were hurt."

Kyle lifted his head. "Did you try to kill Mum?"

Shocked silence filled the kitchen. Tara, horrified and blindsided, stared at her brother. She thought his lower lip quivered a fraction, but his face was firm.

Why's he challenging them? Is he still high on adrenaline from the cougar? It's like his allotment of courage from the last ten years finally caught up to him.

"What?" May tried to smile, but the expression was warped. "Sweetheart, why would you think—"

"You cut the brake's wire. You wanted the crash to be fatal, but it only put her in a coma." Kyle's voice shook, but Tara thought it was from anger more than fear. "You've been following us for ages. I remember seeing Peter outside my room. Go on—try to deny it."

May and Peter looked at each other. His expression was resigned. She lifted a hand to her throat as fresh tears trickled over her cheeks.

"You're half-right," Peter said at last. "We've been trying to meet you since you were born. But we had nothing to do with the crash."

"We *love* Christine," May said. Her face twisted up with long-held pain. "I never wanted to see her hurt."

Kyle kept silent. His fingers gripped the edge of the table, their knuckles white, as he glowered at his grandparents.

Peter sighed, gulped down half of his coffee, put the cup back on the table, and folded his arms. "Your mother left us when she was seventeen. We weren't expecting it; we woke up one morning to find her room empty and a note on her bed: *I never want to see you again.* It broke our hearts. Nearly killed May; her heart isn't so good, and the doctors keep telling her to avoid stress."

"Why'd Mum leave?" Tara asked.

May's head was bowed over her folded hands. "Because of me.

I was terrified that someone or something would hurt my girl. I watched her closely, always. I now see I was smothering her. But at the time, all I wanted was to make sure she never came to harm." She lifted her head and smiled despite red-rimmed eyes. "I vowed to myself that if she gave me another chance, things would be different. But she never came back."

"We looked for her for years," Peter continued. "We didn't want to drag her home. We just wanted to be a part of her life. It took a long time to find her. When we did, we found she'd had children. You two. We wrote to her; she didn't reply. So I went to visit."

Tara leaned forward. "So Kyle *did* see you outside our window. It wasn't a dream."

"That's right." He shrugged. "I wanted to meet my grandchildren. But your mother didn't want that to happen. She moved you away before we could talk. We were starting to fear that reconciliation would be impossible."

Kyle's face remained stony, and he held the death-grip on the table's edge. "How'd you know about the accident?"

"A friend works at the hospital." May traced patterns across the tablecloth as she smiled through her tears. "She recognized Chris's name and called us. We knew Chris wouldn't want us to visit, but we found out you two needed somewhere to stay. We were so, so happy to give you our home."

Do I believe them? Tara examined first May's face and then Peter's. She couldn't find any trace of lies in them—only tiredness and grief.

"I did wrong by your mother," May said, her voice barely above a whisper. "I raised her the way I had been raised. But I'm different now. I prayed for a second chance, and now that I have you two…" She took a quick breath. "I won't make the same mistakes. I won't make you hate me."

Tara looked down at her hot chocolate. The marshmallows had melted into a flat, pillowy layer over the surface. She took a sip; it was bordering on too sweet.

"Do you understand?" May's long fingers shook as she knotted them together. "Are you disappointed in me?"

"No," Tara said quickly. She looked at Kyle for confirmation, but his eyes hadn't left the table. "Thank you for explaining. I think… I think I'd like to go back to bed, if you don't mind."

May made a faint noise, but Peter pressed her shoulder. "Let the kids get some sleep," he said. "We can talk more tomorrow."

"Yes." She rose and moved around the table to kiss both of their foreheads. "Get some rest, my dears. Sleep in as late as you like. I'll cook you a special breakfast when you get up."

She and Peter stood at the base of the stairs and smiled at them as they climbed. Tara waited until they were inside Kyle's room and the door was firmly closed before releasing a held breath. "What are you thinking?"

"They have answers for everything." He flopped onto the edge of the bed. "But they didn't explain the pay phone being down."

"It was a big storm. Probably a bunch of lines went out."

He scowled. "So you trust them now, huh?"

"I…don't know." She rubbed at her exposed forearms. "I

suppose I trust them more than I did before. But maybe not completely. What about you?"

Kyle scuffed his slippers over the carpet then kicked them off and rolled into bed. "I don't know what to think anymore. I just want to sleep."

"Yeah. Me, too. Good night."

CHAPTER 20
IN THE GARDEN

TARA STARTLED AWAKE. SHE blinked at the wood ceiling as disorientation fogged her brain and unnerving dreams sifted away from her conscience. Kyle was still sleeping. The room seemed too dark for it to be morning, but when she looked at Kyle's alarm clock, she saw it was nearly ten.

Heavy gray clouds blocked out the sunlight. Tara rolled out of bed, wrapped her arms around herself to protect against the lingering chill, and went to the window.

Patches of frost lingered over the lawn. Birds fluttered through the forest trees, their shrill screams blending into the rustle of leaves. A figure stood in Peter's garden, surrounded by the sprouts and empty pickets. His shoulders were bowed by age, and his grizzled face was turned toward Tara's window. He made eye contact with Tara then pointed toward the ground. The frost hung over the garden bed like glistening spiderwebs. As he pointed, parts of it melted away. The patches of brown grew and merged to spell a word: HELP. The ghost looked back up at Tara then faded away like smoke in a breeze.

Tara pressed a hand over her mouth. The frost continued to melt until the word disappeared and the garden bed returned to an empty patch of dirt. *Is he asking for help or offering it? Either way can't be a good sign, surely?*

Tara turned from the window and rubbed her hands over the back of her neck. *Maybe I can ask May.* Tara pulled on her dressing gown and, moving quietly so that she wouldn't disturb Kyle, crept into the hall and down the stairs.

May and Peter were already in the kitchen. They spoke quietly, but the words floated through the still house. May was talking about repainting one of the damaged parts of the house, with Peter agreeing occasionally. Then he said, "How long do you want me to wait to reconnect the phone?"

Tara froze. From where she stood, she could barely see May's back as the woman worked in the kitchen. Her shoulders shrugged. "Give it a few more days. Perhaps a week. I'm sure I can bring them around with a bit more time."

Oh no. Tara held her breath. Her sweaty palms stuck to the banister as she crept backward, retreating up the stairs.

Peter said, "All right, just tell me when."

This is bad. Tara didn't dare inhale until she'd reached the hall. She rolled her feet to minimize the noise as she snuck back to Kyle's room and eased the door closed. *It doesn't matter if they're benevolent or even well meaning. This is proof that they're deliberately keeping us isolated.*

She leaned her back against the door and ran a hand over her mouth as she thought. *We've got to leave. Or at least have a way to contact someone…* The memory of the ghost standing in the garden gave her an idea. She crossed to the bed, where her brother continued to sleep. "Kyle."

He stirred at the sound of his name, and Tara nudged his shoulder until he rolled over and squinted at her. "What?"

"Wake up. I have a plan."

He sat up and scratched his scalp, blinking furiously. "A plan for what?"

"To get our phones back. I overheard May and Peter talking about not reconnecting the landline. I'm pretty sure they won't want to give us our phones, but we have to get them. We need a way to contact the outside world."

Alertness returned to Kyle's face. He shuffled onto his knees. "Okay. Go ahead."

"I tried to get the phones from the kitchen last night—but they're not there anymore. I'm pretty sure May moved them into one of the locked rooms. Maybe her bedroom. Which means we need the keys and time alone to search."

"Which we're not going to get." Kyle nodded toward their door. "They'll be watching us like hawks."

"I know. But I think we can get their guard down by voluntarily spending more time with them."

"Which is the exact opposite of getting time alone."

Tara rapped the side of Kyle's head. "Hear the plan out, doofus. This morning, during breakfast, we're going to ask if we can help in the garden. Make it sound like a family bonding event so that May comes, not just Peter. Once we're all outside, I'll say I have a headache and ask to lie down."

His eyes lit up. "And they'll stay outside with me while you nab the keys and go searching."

"Bingo." Tara brushed stray strands of hair out of her face. "The only problem is this goes directly against our promise of sticking together."

"Can't be helped. The keys are on the hook by the kitchen, and May seems to spend her life in there. She'd notice if they went missing. We've got to get her and Peter both outside—and keep them there—if we have a hope of finding our phones." He chewed on the corner of his thumb. "So. Straight after breakfast?"

"Works for me."

They took turns showering. By the time they arrived downstairs, it was closer to lunch than breakfast, but both Peter and May were still in the kitchen.

"Good morning, children." May wore the same hopeful, slightly nervous expression she'd had the night before. "I made you pancakes. Fruit salad and fresh yogurt. Toast and bacon and eggs. And some muffins have just come out of the oven."

"Wow." It was a mountain of food. Tara tried to look excited as she took her seat. "This is incredible, Grandma May."

May beamed. "You had such a bad night last night, I thought you two deserved something special this morning."

Peter watched them as he sipped his coffee, his expression unreadable, and Tara focused on looking carefree and happy as she poured syrup over the pancakes.

Kyle cleared his throat. "I was thinking… I need a hobby other than books. Something to do outdoors. Do you think Tara and I could help in the garden? It'd be nice to have our own plants we can water and watch grow."

Genius, Kyle. May's expression brightened, and she nudged Peter's shoulder as she moved past. "That sounds lovely, doesn't it, Peter? The kids can have their own sections in the garden."

"Yeah." Tara tried to build on the image. "Grandpa Peter said you like flowers, May. Why don't you have a corner, too? We can all grow different things. It'll be a family garden."

For a second, she worried she'd pushed too far, but May only laughed. "I'd like that. What do you say, Peter? Ready to relinquish your hold on the ground out back?"

He snorted, but the corners of his mouth twitched up. "I'd be glad for some help."

"Let's start this morning," Tara said. "While it's nice out."

"All right," May said indulgently. "But finish your breakfast first."

Tara and Kyle exchanged a smile. They ate quickly. Nerves had wormed their way into Tara's stomach and unsettled it, but not wanting May to think she was unhappy, she finished her plate. Peter disappeared into the house to find them work gloves while May washed up, then together, they stepped into the overcast day.

Peter carried a small toolbox and a canvas sack of implements, which he dropped at the side of the garden. He handed out shovels then cracked open the toolbox. It was full of packets of seeds.

"Pick what you like," he said, indicating different sections. "Flowers here. Root vegetables, lettuces, and squash here. Got a couple of types of tomatoes."

"No fruit?" Tara asked, kneeling beside the crate.

"We've got strawberries, but it's better to buy most fruits as saplings. Dig some trenches today, then tell me what you want, and I'll get them at a nursery."

Tara took the pack of strawberries as well as cucumbers and lettuces. Kyle knelt over the box, his face scrunched up in concentration as he chose his plants. May watched and smiled as Peter divided the prepared ground into sections and showed Tara how to use the shovel. She'd meant for the garden to be a quick distraction, but Tara found herself growing increasingly enthusiastic about her little plot as she dug rows.

She allowed just enough time for it to be convincing then scrunched up her face and leaned over her shovel. May, who had done very little work and mostly watched, moved forward. "Is something wrong, honey?"

"Just a headache." She shook her head and blinked. "I'm probably still tired from last night."

May pressed the back of her hand to Tara's forehead, a frown pulling at her eyes. "Would you like a glass of water? You might be dehydrated."

"Nah, it'll be fine. I just get headaches sometimes."

"Maybe you should lie down. We can always come back to the garden later."

Bingo. "That sounds really good, actually. You guys keep going. I'll catch up with you later."

"I'll make you a cup of tea and a warm compress," May said, starting toward the house with her hand on Tara's shoulder.

"Thanks, but…but—" Caught off guard, Tara desperately hunted for an excuse that would sound convincing. "Please stay with Kyle. He gets lonely so easily. Would you keep him company while I can't?"

May's eyes flicked over Tara's face for a second, then she smiled and nodded. "Of course. Have something to drink. I'll call you when dinner's ready."

As May returned to the garden, Kyle gave Tara a quick nod. Tara nodded back, wishing him luck. She kept a slow pace until the house's front door closed behind her, then she snatched the keys off the hook by the door. Kyle would keep their grandparents in the garden for as long as he could, but there was no guarantee of how long that might be. She needed to be quick.

Where would May hide the phones? From Tara's count, there were at least six locked doors in the house. She bit her lower lip as she jogged up the stairs to the second floor. *Maybe in the master bedroom. It's the last on the right, isn't it?*

Tara tried the door handle and wasn't surprised when it didn't turn. She counted her breaths as she sorted through the keys. There were twenty of them, and it took too long for comfort to find the right one. At last, a bronze key turned in the lock, and a soft click let her twist the handle.

The room wasn't what she'd expected. Flowing white curtains and blue-patterned wallpaper matched May's style, but the bed was a single, not double. *Does Peter sleep in a different room? They seem so close. Maybe he snores?*

She tucked the keys into her back pocket and began searching. The room was pin-neat, so Tara took excruciating care to put things back the way they'd been. She hunted through the dresser drawers, the top shelf of the wardrobe, the bedside table drawers, and even looked under the bed for a secret compartment without any luck. As she straightened, laughter floated through the window. Being careful not to be seen, Tara crept up to the glass and peeked outside.

The garden bed was nearly directly below the window. Kyle was clowning it up and waving the shovel around like a sword while May and Peter laughed. The scene looked happy—almost whimsical—and Tara felt a small pang of regret for what could have been. She rubbed at her arm as she prepared to leave the room.

She sensed the ghost's presence before she saw it. The room seemed to grow a fraction dimmer, and an icy chill floated over Tara's arm. She sucked in a breath as she turned. Two pit-black eyes stared back at her.

CHAPTER 21
FAMILY

THE DEAD WOMAN'S FACE, framed by thick steel-gray hair, was as sunken as her husband's. She tilted her head to one side, and for a moment, she looked as real and tangible as any living human. Then her form flickered into transparency as she reached a hand toward Tara.

Tara stumbled backward, a hand pressed over her mouth to muffle a scream. Her legs gave out, and she collapsed to the floor. She scrambled away from the specter, not stopping until her back hit the wall.

The woman was old—older than May—and a dark mourning gown swirled around her in an invisible wind. Her dark eyes followed Tara's movements as her form continued to bleed away, making her appear fainter with every passing second.

"I'm sorry," Tara said, although she wasn't sure what she was apologizing for.

The ghost extended her hand toward the desk below the window. She rested her fingertips on a thick, leather-bound book, her gaze never wavering from Tara. Then her form evaporated, disappearing into the ether, and the oppressive, suffocating gloom lifted from the room.

Tara kept still for several long moments. She kept waiting for the specter to return. When it didn't, she slowly crawled to her knees and lifted herself onto unsteady feet.

I need to get out of this room. The phones aren't here. I don't know how much time I have, but the keys need to be back on the hook when May comes inside.

She hesitated, though. The ghost had touched the book on the writing desk. *Was it trying to show me something?* Uneasiness made her skin prickle as she approached the book, feeling more wary than curious.

The leather cover was blank, but the shape—wider than it was tall—told her it was a photo album. Wearing around the edges and corners suggested it was frequently opened. Tara pulled the cover back. Inside were dozens of black-and-white photos, arranged neatly, with small cursive writing under each picture. *The Folcroft family at the lake, Summer 1933. Harry works the garden, 1928. Christopher, age four, helps Eileen bake a pie.*

Tara stopped at a familiar face. The girl from the lake stared up at her balefully, a white cloth with a tree design held toward the camera. *Anna Folcroft learns embroidery.*

She turned the page. A large photo took up so much space that the names had to be squeezed into the bottom margin. It was a family portrait, with two adults and five children arranged in various sitting and standing poses. *Harry, Eileen, Anna, Peter, Christopher, and May Folcroft.*

Tara's mouth dried. The picture was all wrong. The faces were familiar—the man, Harry, had stood in the garden that morning, and Eileen's face was a younger version of the ghost that had shown Tara the book. But the names didn't match the gravestones hidden behind the house.

May cares about family deeply—but the path to the graves is never used. Is it possible Petra and George aren't relatives? Do we have strangers' graves on this land?

Another anomaly hit her as she looked at the last child, May Folcroft. Her hair hung in ringlets around her head as she clutched a doll to her chest. *But May married into the family. How could she be in this picture?*

Confusion and growing dread rose through Tara. She took a step back from the book, hands pressed to her forehead. The door behind her creaked as it opened, and Tara gasped.

"And here you are." A heavy sadness weighted down May's voice. "It would have been better if you'd stayed away, my dear."

Tara couldn't speak. She could only stare in horror as May closed the door with a sharp snap. The woman crossed to the book, moving so close to Tara that she could smell the cinnamon scent that seemed to hang around her. May's long fingers touched the photo reverently then closed the book.

"You have probably realized I am not Peter's wife. I am his sister. And Christine is not our child."

Tara's throat was too dry to swallow. She backed away from May until she hit the wall. "I don't understand."

May braced her hands on the table. She looked tired. A breeze fluttered the curtains around her, hiding her face for brief moments. When she spoke, it was with thick resignation. "There is nothing more important to us than family. Things are different now, but back when I was young, it was expected that women would marry and move in with their new husband. The idea always repulsed me. Why would I commit my life to a stranger when I had everything I needed at home? I trusted my family. I relied on them, and they on me. We had a harmony that no suitor could hope to rival."

She paused to breathe. Tara stayed pressed against the wall, afraid to move or speak in case it provoked some form of retaliation. But when May finally looked at her, it was with a smile.

"During the war, our family withdrew from society. We barely went into town. Most people didn't even know our names. Over several decades, our parents and siblings died—by drowning, illness, and old age. Eventually, only Peter and I remained. We were happy together. He took care of the garden, I managed the house, and our parents had left enough savings that we would never need jobs.

"One day, a family arrived at our house. A young man, his wife, and their baby. They were hiding because of some very bad things they'd done during the war." May's fingers traced over the book's leather cover. "I told them government officials were coming. I said I would look after their baby while they hid in the bunker."

"Oh…no…" Sickness and horror churned in Tara's stomach.

"Don't worry, sweetheart. They didn't suffer. They probably didn't even realize they were suffocating." May's smile was shaky, bordering on desperate. "We gave them good, respectful burials. Peter carved the gravestones: one each for George Kendall and Petra Kendall."

Kendall. Our surname. A morbid fascination was growing through Tara's fear. *This must be what Mum found out on the day she ran away, when she wrote about secrets in her journal. She adopted her birth parents' surname.*

May took a short, shallow breath. "We renamed their baby Christine. It had been so long since anyone in town had seen us that they naturally assumed we were a married couple when we took our daughter to the doctor. That suited us. People used to say our family was strange for being so close. But no one questions a married couple growing old together. Isn't that ridiculous?"

Her laughter made shivers creep up Tara's spine.

"We're not bad people, Tara," May said as her chuckles died. "We only led those strangers to the bunker because it was the right thing to do. They were sick. Not physically, but in their minds; it was like a rot that would grow worse and worse every day. We did it to save your mother. We did it for Christine."

You're lying. Tara bit her tongue to keep the words inside. She no longer had any doubt that Peter had tampered with Chris's car brakes. She was starting to understand how obsessed May was with family…and how far she would go to have one.

"You understand, don't you, my dear?" May's long fingers brushed hair away from Tara's face. They felt strangely cold. "We did it for the best. And we loved Christine—just like we love you and Kyle. We'll take care of you. We'll cherish you."

When Tara didn't speak, May pulled her close, pressing Tara's head into the space below her chin. "I know this is a shock, my darling. But I know you'll understand when you think it through a bit. You're not like your mother; she was stubborn and willful. She didn't understand the type of family we are. But you do, I'm sure. You know what's best for you and your brother."

From where May held her, Tara could see the garden. Kyle and Peter still worked in it. Kyle sent a terrified glance toward the house.

"You don't want anything bad to happen to him." May's breath tickled the top of Tara's head as she whispered into her hair. The fingers kept moving, running up and down Tara's shoulder and refusing to let her pull away. "You don't want him to be hurt. You'll be a good girl, won't you?"

Fear turned Tara's stomach cold. The smell of cinnamon surrounded her. She could barely breathe, but when she did, she said, "Yes."

"Yes," May echoed, and Tara felt the woman smile against her hair. "You *are* a good girl. So different from Chris. *You're* not going to break your grandmother's heart."

Kyle looked back toward the house, his face sheet white and perspiration dripping off his forehead.

"Good girl," May cooed, her fingers tightening on Tara's arms.

"Now, my dear, you have a headache, don't you? You'd better take that lie-down."

May eased her away from the photo album and into the hallway. Tara wanted to push out of her arms and reject the repulsive embrace, but she couldn't. Not as long as they had Kyle.

"Sleep as long as you like." May finally released Tara when they were inside her room. She was smiling, but the expression didn't touch her eyes. "Don't worry about coming down for dinner. I'll bring it to you."

She pulled the key ring from Tara's pocket and shut the door. There was silence for a beat, then the lock clicked.

Tara covered her mouth. A high-pitched ringing noise filled her skull as terrified tears ran over her cheeks.

CHAPTER 22
WAITING GAMES

TARA PACED THE ROOM, running her hands over her face and through her hair as she raced to piece together a plan.

As long as Kyle and I can get to town, we should be safe. But the drive was long, and the trip would be longer by foot. They either needed transport or a head start at a time when they wouldn't be missed for hours.

They're not going to leave us alone for hours, though. May is smarter than I anticipated if she saw through the gardening diversion. So that means we need a car.

She didn't have a license, but her mother had let her try driving the car around an abandoned parking lot one night. She thought she could handle the Jeep as far as the town. But actually getting the Jeep wouldn't be easy. The key was on the key ring, and she suspected the metal band wouldn't be left out of eyesight any time soon.

And even if I had a way to get the keys—even if we had a chance to make a run for it—I can't do anything until I'm out of this room. How long will she keep me here? Just tonight? A few days? And when I'm let out, how long will it take to gain enough trust to be left unsupervised, or to even talk to Kyle in private?

Tara gritted her teeth against a moan as she keeled over onto the bed. There was too much risk. If she tried to make a break for it and was caught, she dreaded what they would do to Kyle. May had her bunker. Peter had his rifle. And they had both killed—or attempted to kill—before.

The overcast sky turned the light filtering into her room gray. Tara rolled off the bed and approached the window. She tried the latch. The frame wouldn't budge—it was either frozen from age, or intentionally locked. The panes were big, though. Tara thought she could break the glass and crawl through.

Movement outside pulled her eyes to the yard. Peter's tall frame moved slowly and smoothly, circling the house. He tilted his head to glance at Tara's window as he passed, and the weak sunlight glinted off the rifle cocked over his elbow.

Tara shrank back from the window as nausea built up inside of her again. They weren't going to tolerate any form of resistance. She hoped Kyle was smart enough not to confront them. *If either of those monsters hurt him, I'll kill them.*

She squeezed her clammy hands into fists. Her powerlessness was like a prickling thorn in her chest, and every second she sat made it worse.

Don't be rash. Don't make things worse.

Peter wouldn't stay awake forever. Once the house was fully silent, she could escape and get Kyle, and they would make a break for it. She imagined running down the driveway in the middle of the night, tripping over the potholes and swiping at scratching branches, praying all the way that headlights wouldn't appear behind them.

The prickling thorn felt worse. She squeezed her eyes shut and pressed her hands over the lids to block out all traces of sunlight. Instead of thinking about the escape, she tried to focus on their life afterward.

They would be able to go home. Kyle would have his vast library, and the computer would restore the friendships Tara was desperately missing. They would have their own beds again. The chewy honey cereal Kyle loved. The fishbowl with Nemo, their calico goldfish.

Except we can't go back there. May and Peter know where we live. They have to—that's how they tampered with Mum's car. Which means we'll need to go on the run. Change our names. Move far enough away that we can't be found and cut off all of our friendships.

But at least we'll be able to see Mum again…assuming she's still alive.

The thorn hurt so badly that she wanted to scream. She leaped up and attacked her pillow, pummeling it with both fists as whispered cries leaked out between her clenched teeth. When her arms were so tired that the punches stopped being satisfying, Tara collapsed onto the bed and rolled over so that she no longer faced the window. She knew she would need to stay up through the night, so she tried to sleep. It was a hopeless cause when her anxiety was wound up so high and the frustrated thorn continued to prickle.

Day slowly collapsed. As the sunset painted violent red colors across the angry clouds, footsteps approached her door. Tara sat up as May entered, carrying a tray. "Hello, my dear. I hope you're feeling better. I brought you your dinner."

I could kill her. The thought came out of nowhere but didn't retreat. *She's old. She's frail. I could smash her head between the door and its frame. I could press my pillow over her face and keep it there as she gasps. I could wrap my bed sheets around her neck and cinch them tight. And then I'd be a murderer…just like she is.*

May placed the tray on the bedside table. If she had any idea of the thoughts running through Tara's head, she didn't show it. Instead, she caressed hair away from Tara's face. "This has been a very stressful time for you. But things will get better. I promise. We're taking good care of Kyle." She sighed. The creases on her face looked deeper and grayer than normal, and even though she smiled, it was a pained expression. "Excuse me, my dear. It's been a long day; I might go to bed early, too. Sleep well."

The door clicked closed. Tara released the sheets from her grip and looked toward the tray. She had been given stew, warm bread, a cup of tea, fresh salad, apple cubes, and even a slice of cake. There was enough to feed three of her. She didn't touch any of it.

Tara sat up in bed, waiting, as the last crimson stains bled out of the sky. She didn't turn her light on. If she was lucky, May and Peter would think she'd fallen asleep. She kept as still as she could, hands holding on to the brightly colored quilt, and listened to the building.

Voices came from downstairs, their words warped and jumbled until they were indistinguishable. Footsteps moved through the house. A pipe rattled as someone washed their hands or brushed their teeth in the bathroom down the hall. Tara hoped it was Kyle. He would be terrified. If May had given him an excuse for Tara's absence, she knew he wouldn't believe it.

The footsteps left the bathroom and approached her door. Then Peter's voice said, "Time for bed." The footsteps stopped, turned, and retreated to the room two doors away from her. Peter followed. Tara barely made out the sound of a lock clicking as Kyle's door was secured. Then silence returned to the house when Peter went back downstairs.

She waited while the night animals woke up and started screeching in the woods behind her. Peter looped around the house twice in the following hour; his footsteps were stealthy but still loud enough to hear. Sometime around midnight, a door closed downstairs.

Tara kept waiting, nerves keeping her alert despite the progressing hours. She was cold but kept still, not wanting to make any noises until the Folcroft family was fully asleep.

When her alarm clock said it was half past two, she finally stood and pulled a heavy jacket over her shivering limbs. She was aware of how much noise every motion made. The rustle of her jacket, the subtle groan of floorboards under her feet, even her breathing seemed unnaturally loud. She went to the window.

Breaking the glass would make too much noise. Tara braced her foot against the wardrobe and leveraged her body weight and her muscles against the frame. It groaned, then the wood cracked, and it burst open.

Tara caught herself on the sill. She held her position there, breathing shallowly, as she waited to see if anyone had heard. Minutes ticked by. The house remained quiet.

The moon was large and bright enough to let her see, even with the cloud cover dimming it. Tara examined the house wall. The window to her right was less than ten feet away. A narrow ledge of protruding stones ran along the wall, marking the point where the first floor ended and the second began. Tara squeezed her lips together and swung her leg through the open window.

She hadn't expected how difficult it would be to reach a foot onto the ledge without falling off the sill. For one awful second, she thought she was trapped with one leg still inside the room and the rest of her body out, but then she heaved herself through the opening. Her toes touched the stone protrusion. She eased her weight onto it until her arms were only holding the window-sill for balance.

Why did my hobby have to be blogs? Why couldn't it have been rock climbing or jujitsu?

The ground looked dizzyingly far below. A fall from the second floor probably wouldn't kill her, but she doubted she could escape it without broken bones. She focused her attention on the window ten feet away and began shuffling along the ledge.

The protrusion was only large enough for her toes to rest on.

It wasn't too bad while she could brace herself on the window, but as she edged farther along the ledge, balancing became difficult. She pressed her body as close to the wall as possible, keeping her stomach pulled in and her breaths shallow as her spread fingers ran along the rough stone surface.

Don't stop. Don't look down.

Her calves cramped. It was becoming harder and harder to press herself into the wall. Her fingers scrambled ineffectively, hunting for any sort of hold she could dig her nails into.

Left foot moves out. Shift your weight. Right foot pulls in.

The windowsill was only a couple of feet away. Her initial plan had been to pass it and keep moving to Kyle's room, but she was starting to realize her legs wouldn't carry her. She would have to stop in the locked room—even if for just a couple of minutes.

Her outstretched hand found the sill. She grabbed it, thankful for something to occupy her fingers with, and shuffled closer. In her eagerness, she moved too quickly. Her left foot plunged off the ledge. Tara didn't even have time to take a breath as she fell. Her side hit the windowsill, and she clutched at it.

She came to a stop with one foot still straining to hold her on the ledge, and her upper body clinging to the sill. Her heart thundered in her ears. She didn't know if she'd screamed, or, if she had, how loud it had been.

Slowly and carefully, Tara pulled herself onto the ledge. She was surprised and relieved to find the window was open a crack. The hinges groaned as the panes turned, but then she was able to climb over the sill and collapse inside the room.

She lay on the floor as she caught her breath and waited for her shaking legs to recover. Her shoulder and ribs hurt where they'd hit the stones, but at least she was inside. Even better, she couldn't hear any movement in the house.

Tara pushed herself up then squinted to make out the space in the moon's glow. Everything was smothered in shadows except the glint of blue light on a pair of bright eyes.

CHAPTER 23
THE LOCKED ROOM

TARA COULDN'T MAKE A sound. She pressed her back into the wall as her heart missed a beat. The eyes, pit-black, stared down at her. Then they blinked and faded into nothing. *Just a ghost. That's all.*

She'd never thought she would be relieved to see a spirit. Tara clamped a hand over her mouth to quiet her frantic breathing. Her fingers were numb from cold, and her head buzzed with the stress. She waited in case the ghost reappeared, but the room stayed still.

The space was crowded with old wooden furniture. Shelves and wardrobes covered the walls, and large wingback armchairs were arranged in a circle in the center of the room. Strange, lumpy shapes had been arranged in the chairs, almost like human-sized dolls. Tara shifted forward, her curiosity winning out over nerves.

The shapes had been wrapped in blankets and propped against the chairs' sides. Only their outlines were visible in the dark. As

Tara crept closer, she thought she could see curled hair poking out from the nearest bundle.

She looked down. Shoes had been laid on the ground in front of each chair: a pair of boots by the nearest and smaller women's shoes in front of the one past it. As she lifted her eyes, light caught on a gold wedding ring threaded around a skeletal finger.

Tara's whole body convulsed as a near-silent whine escaped her. The lumpy shapes nestled in the blankets were skulls propped on top of collapsing skeletons.

"You're too curious."

Tara swiveled so quickly that she hit one of the chairs, making the skeleton huddled in it rattle. She stepped back, wide eyes fixed on the shadowed chair where May sat. The older woman reclined with her hands braced on the armrests. Tara couldn't detect any anger in her face, but there was an awful, overwhelming finality in her expression.

"I have forgiven you time and time again. I have tried—" Her voice broke, and she took a shuddering breath to steady it. "I have tried so, so hard to be a good grandmother. I took you in, though you weren't my flesh and blood. I fed you. Bought you gifts. And you've repaid me only in insolence." Her mouth tightened, and the wrinkles that had once looked so cheerful seemed to be severe lines.

Tara couldn't control her shaking. She knew she was stuttering, but the words spilled out in an uncontrolled rush. "W-we didn't ask for any of that. We didn't sign up to be a part of your crazy family. We didn't ask you to s-sabotage Mum's car. And we de-definitely didn't ask for *this* insanity." She thrust a hand toward the shriveled shapes in the chairs.

"Hah." May's expression softened a fraction. "This was my mother's idea, initially. My younger brother, Christopher, died before his fifth birthday. She couldn't bear to bury him. To leave him encased in cold, wet dirt while worms and insects disintegrated him… She found the concept intolerable. So she wrapped him in his favorite blanket and kept him in the spare room. That way, he could stay warm and dry and surrounded by people who loved him."

Tara swallowed the bile that rose in her throat. She wrapped her arms around herself, sickened to even be in the building.

May's slow, soft voice continued, its easy cadence at odds with the words. "When my father died, she did the same. She would sit with him in this very chair every evening. She wanted to keep him company, she said. And, finally, on Mother's passing, Peter asked me if I wanted to bury her. I did not." She reached a hand to the chair to her right and caressed the exposed arm bone. "I've gotten used to seeing their ghosts. Normally, they don't appear often—they've been more active since you've been here—but it was a comfort to know they hadn't left. Not really."

A sickening idea occurred to Tara. "They can't rest unless they're buried."

"I think you're right." May's whisper-soft voice held notes of delight. Her eyes shone in the moonlight as she smiled up at Tara. "Your mother's parents never showed themselves once we gave them graves."

"This is wrong." Tara's back hit the wall. "You're demented."

May only smiled. "Am I? All I ever wanted was to keep my family close. I was robbed of my sweet little Christine, but now I have you and Kyle to take her place. Don't worry. You'll learn to be happy here soon enough. Kyle is already taking steps in the right direction."

"What did you do to him?" The anxious, helpless thorny feeling was digging at her insides again and making her want to scream.

"He was being quite stubborn." May tilted her head to the side, as carefree as if she were discussing the weather. "He broke out of his room. So I took him somewhere more secure. He'll be much more settled after a night in the bunker."

No. No. No. No. The scream built but strangled in Tara's throat. She understood May was distracting her; the slow, easy monologue was erasing precious seconds, each one costing Kyle more oxygen.

Tara dashed past the swaddled corpses and grabbed at the door's handle. It was locked, so she slammed her body into it, no longer caring who heard. It didn't budge, so she stepped farther back and hit it hard enough to bruise her whole side. She cried out in relief when the lock broke and the door banged open.

She didn't wait to see if May was following. Her legs carried her to the end of the hallway and down the stairs three at a time. Her pace was too hectic. She tripped over the last stairs, hit the ground hard, scrambled back to her feet, and kept moving.

By a miracle, the key ring was still on the hook beside the kitchen. She yanked it off hard enough to bend the metal then burst out the front door.

Long grass swayed in the icy breeze. Its color had been distorted by the moonlight, and the motion made it look like an undulating ocean. Tara aimed herself toward the bunker's concrete entrance and ran as fast as her legs could move her.

I can't be too late. How long has he been in there? How long until he runs out of oxygen? How long until brain damage?

Tears stung her cheeks, and her breathing became labored, but she didn't slow until she hit the bunker's door with a heavy clang. "Kyle? Kyle, I'm here!"

She fumbled the keys. The first one didn't fit. The second wouldn't turn. She sifted through them, trying each shape in turn, her mind being swallowed by panic as seconds passed without a reply.

The fifth key worked. She wrenched the door open and jogged down the stairs, one hand running over the concrete wall and the other held ahead of her. She stumbled as the stairs evened out into the hallway. Another four steps forward, and her hand hit a wall. "Kyle?"

A door creaked, then slammed. The sound shook the room and left a dull, reverberating echo to fill the space long after the original noise faded. Fear hit Tara. She turned back, feeling her way toward the stairs, but her hand hit the cold metal of a door instead. "No—"

The bulb above her head hissed as it turned on. Tara swiveled to face the tiny room. May sat in the chair against the opposite wall, her long fingers clasped on her lap.

"Wh—" Tara shook her head. "Where's Kyle?"

"Not here." She exhaled, looking pleased with herself, and reached her hands toward Tara. Even though they were at opposite ends of the room, Tara had to press herself into the door to avoid the touch. "It's funny, you know. You're angry with me now, but deep down, we're so much alike."

"We're nothing alike," Tara spat. Her chest hurt from the run, and her head buzzed with stress. All she wanted to do was collapse onto the floor, but she kept her feet.

"Oh, but we are. Look at how quickly you ran here on the mere suggestion that Kyle was in danger. You love your family just as much as I do."

"You're *not* my family."

May's smile cracked. She stared at Tara, and an intense, near-fanatical light seemed to shine in her eyes. When she spoke, it was clearly an effort to keep her voice soft and warm. "Let's not argue tonight. I don't like seeing you distressed."

Tara nearly choked on her fury. "Well, it's *your fault* if I am!"

"Shh. Be calm, my dear. I want your last hours to be peaceful."

The gravity of the situation finally registered. Tara gaped at May for a second then turned and felt for a handle to open the door. There wasn't one; instead, a small keyhole waited for a key—the key that would be on the key ring she'd left in the upper door.

"Let me out," Tara said. She fought to keep her voice level.

"I wouldn't even if I was able to." May rose and took a step closer. Tara refused to look at her, but she could feel the older woman hovering just behind her shoulder. "Believe me. It's better this way. I'll stay with you until it's over. I can sing to you, if you like."

Tara rested her head against the door. She was painfully aware of her breathing. She was using the air too fast, but her lungs didn't want to slow. "You'll die, too."

"It's a little too late for that, I'm afraid." May laughed as Tara turned toward her.

The woman's form didn't seem as solid as it had before. Her white nightdress swirled in a wind that didn't exist. She extended a hand to caress Tara's shoulder, and the touch was like an icy wind.

Tara licked her lips. "You're dead."

"Very recently, yes." May sighed. "My heart has been giving me trouble for such a long time. I knew I didn't have long, which was why I asked Peter to…to *take care* of your mother. I wanted to have a family around me again, even if just for a short time."

Tara struggled to inject confidence into her words. "Not trying to lie about the accident anymore, huh?"

"No. There's no point now. I had hoped to make you love me…to make you love this house and this family. My will leaves the property to you after my death. You and Kyle could have stayed here, happy and safe, where Peter and I could watch over you every day." May's smile dropped. "But you've been so stubborn. So rebellious. The stress and the frustration were too great to bear. My heart failed last night. And that signaled the end of my opportunity to win your loyalty."

She settled back into the chair, hands folded neatly in her lap, and shrugged. "Now, the only way to keep my family intact is to tie you here. Peter will bring your body to the upstairs family room tomorrow morning. He'll wrap you in a nice warm blanket and arrange you next to your relatives. And we can stay together, living past death, forever."

"No." Tara shook her head, but May only laughed.

"It will be easier if you don't work yourself into a frenzy, my dear. This is not the worst way to die. The carbon monoxide will poison you before you run out of oxygen. It's a gentle end; you'll feel tired and eventually fall asleep. And I'll be here the whole time to keep you company and to comfort you. Are you sure you wouldn't like me to sing?"

The words came out as a whisper. "What about Kyle?"

"He'll join you; don't worry. He's taking a different path to the next life, but you'll be able to see him soon."

May's smile was clearly intended to seem warm and motherly, but in that moment, with the bulb's harsh light warring with the shadows over her semitransparent face, she looked like a wolf.

CHAPTER 24
RESTLESS DEAD

TARA'S LEGS WANTED TO collapse, but she refused to show weakness in front of May. Instead, she kept her back pressed against the door. Her mind raced, but she couldn't see even a sliver of hope. Bargaining wouldn't work when May was getting exactly what she wanted. She didn't have any threats to wield. And even if there was some way to bring May on to her side, the dead woman wasn't physically capable of opening the thick metal door.

She turned back to the structure, her fingers scrabbling over the smooth surface and its indented keyhole. She squirmed a finger inside and tried to pull, but a latch had fixed the door into place.

Her lungs ached. She tried to tell herself it was from fear, not impending suffocation, but her body wasn't convinced. Chilled sweat coated her, and tears burned her eyes.

The metal under her hand felt cold—far colder than it had

been a moment before. Tara pulled her fingers away and frowned as tiny frost crystals appeared on the surface. Then a translucent form broke through the door. Its long nose was inches from Tara's, and she gasped as she staggered back.

May rose out of the chair, her voice suddenly harsh. "Why are you here? What have you done?"

The spirit was familiar. The woman's sunken cheeks were heavily shadowed, and her black mourning dress swirled in a wind that Tara couldn't feel. Her eyes searched Tara's face, and an intense sadness filled their depths. Then they hardened as she looked toward May. The specter's voice was a whisper like long-dead leaves scraping together. "She isn't ready for death."

May laughed. The noise was nearly hysterical. "Is anyone, Mother? Were you?"

"*Death* is not ready for *her*."

Neither spoke for a moment. Eileen's form was weaker than May's. Even while Tara watched, it started to fade as the color bled out of her. May's face froze into hard angles. "What have you done?"

Eileen smiled. Her lips moved, but the words were barely audible. "I am fortunate that my son is not as ruthless as my daughter."

"No," May hissed.

A rhythmic pounding noise became audible through the airtight door. Tara looked from Eileen to the exit, scarcely allowing herself to hope. As the pounding drew nearer, it resolved into heavy footsteps. May clamped her hands over her head and shrieked in frustration and fury.

Metal clanged as a key was fit into the door. It scraped as it turned, then the metal frame pulled open. A gust of fresh air rushed around Tara, and Peter stood in the opening. He looked aged since the last time Tara had seen him; his long face was gray and furrowed by exhaustion. Even so, he smiled as he saw his sister. "Here you are, May. I've been looking for you."

"Don't let the girl escape!" Desperation infused May's words. "You promised, Peter."

"I promised to give you a family one last time. You've had five days with them. That's enough."

"No, please. They can stay with us. I've already taken care of the boy. We only need to leave the girl here—"

"No, May." His voice was sad but firm. "This is enough. You need to let go."

May's eyes flashed with anger. The older ghost, Eileen, appeared behind her. She wrapped her arms around her daughter. Her whisper made shivers crawl up Tara's spine. "Death is not a blessing. Let her go. Let us *all* go. We need to be free, my dear."

"Please—no—" Tears streamed down May's cheeks. She looked between the two of them but didn't try to shake her way out of her mother's arms.

Peter finally glanced at Tara. His expression was unreadable. He nodded toward the stairs. "Go on."

Tara didn't hesitate. She flattened herself against the wall to squeeze past him then dashed up the stairs. Her footsteps echoed off the walls like drumbeats. She drew a gasp as she burst into the yard and dropped to her knees.

Where's Kyle? She said she took care of him. What does that mean? He can't be dead yet—he can't be. She didn't have enough time to kill him, surely.

She forced herself back onto her feet. The house looked strangely alien in the moonlight. Lights were on in a couple of rooms, and they spread blocks of gold across the moon-tinted grass. Tara scanned the windows as she jogged toward the house. She couldn't see any movement inside.

The bunker door screeched as it was closed, but Tara didn't look behind her. She was wholly focused on finding Kyle. Everything else had to come second until then.

As she burst through the door, she was struck by how quiet the house seemed. Outside, she'd been surrounded by animal calls and the trees' whispers. But the house felt *dead*.

"*Kyle!*" She bellowed as loudly as her lungs could manage and began darting through the rooms without waiting for an answer. She took the stairs to the second floor and skidded to a halt at Kyle's room. The door was open. He'd stacked his books at the base of the bed, and his suitcase sat open by the door. It had been hastily filled with clothes.

He was hoping to escape, too.

"Kyle?" She wasn't surprised that there wasn't any answer. The room had the still, sedate atmosphere of a place that hadn't been disturbed in a while. Tara returned to the hallway and shoved open every unlocked door. Some led into empty rooms. Others were spare bedrooms, where the furniture and bedding apparently had been untouched for decades. None held any signs of life.

A floorboard creaked on the lower floor. Tara's heart leaped into her throat as she ran back to the stairs. She stopped on the lower landing. A figure moved down the hallway toward her.

Peter emerged from the shadows, May's body cradled in his arms. She looked impossibly small and frail as her long gray hair shimmered in the lights. Peter didn't even glance toward Tara to acknowledge her before he carried his sister's body past the stairs and through the front door. They disappeared into the night.

Tara's mouth was dry. She backed away from the door then turned to search the lower level. Many of the doors were still locked, but Tara beat her fist on each of them and listened for a response before moving on. The farther she moved, the more she became convinced that Kyle was no longer inside the house.

Where is he? What did May say earlier? "Kyle is already taking steps in the right direction"? She couldn't mean—

Tara ran back into the night, toward the paths wending into the forest. They were unrecognizable at night. She had to guess which one led to the lake.

There wasn't enough time to mind her steps. She stumbled, staggered, and crashed through the trees, her torso bent to help her watch the ground and make sure she didn't stray off the worn path.

Animals howled in the distance. A bird exploded out of the grass between two trees and screamed in terror as it spiraled toward the sky. Tara was gasping, her legs shaking and a headache pounding behind her eyes. She slowed, bent double to catch her breath, then started running again.

The path leveled out. The trees thinned. Then Tara broke through into the clearing, and the lake's water sparkled like a diamond sea ahead.

Kyle was already on the pier. His shadow stretched ahead of him toward the dock's end, where two eyes glowed out of the darkness.

Tara, her heart in her throat, scrambled down the embankment. "Kyle, *wake up!*"

He twitched, but the slow, sluggish paces didn't stop. He was nearly at the dock's end. A long gray hand reached out of the lake and stretched its fingers toward Kyle, as though offering to help him into the water. He extended his own hand to the dripping limb, and the glowing eyes flashed brighter.

Tara caught Kyle's shoulder as he started to topple forward. She threw him back. They hit the wood, and pain flared through Tara's bruised side. She didn't allow herself a chance to rest, but rolled onto her knees to face the pier's end.

The drowned girl's glowing eyes narrowed. Slowly, the extended hand drew back, and the dripping creature submerged itself into the lake's depths.

Tara wrapped her arms around Kyle to keep him grounded. He blinked furiously as confusion and fear alternated over his face. "Wha...where—"

"May's dead." Tara spoke between thin, painful breaths. "The house is full of dead bodies. We're not even related to the Folcrofts. This whole situation is bonkers."

"Was I...sleepwalking?"

"More like sleep lured." She glanced at the still water a final time then tugged on Kyle. "Let's get away from here. I feel like Anna's still watching us."

Kyle got to his feet. They held on to each other as they walked back to solid ground. Tara's legs were still shaking, so she collapsed onto the dirt once they were far enough away from the shore for her to feel safe. She ran her hands over her face. "I'm glad you're okay."

"Same." His face was pale and serious as he sat cross-legged at her side and watched the water. "I'm really, really sorry. I tried to stop May from going back inside, but—"

"It's okay. She was—is—smarter than I gave her credit for."

Kyle worried at his lip then said, "What are we going to do?"

"I don't know." Tara lifted her eyes toward the starry sky. The clouds were dispersing, and the moon broke through, bright and clear. "I really, really have no idea. I'm sorry."

"We'll be together, though, won't we?"

"Yeah." She reached out and gripped his clammy fingers. "We'll stick together."

She was so tired, she thought she could fall asleep there, even with sticks and rocks poking her back. The relief of finding Kyle had drained the adrenaline out of her system and left her shaky and dizzy. Kyle seemed to understand and let her sit in silence for several minutes. Then he turned toward the woods' edge. "Did you hear that?"

Tara sat up as sick dread built in her stomach. "What was it?"

"Like footsteps or something."

Heavy, slow steps moved in their direction, crunching leaves and snapping sticks. Too heavy and loud for a mountain lion or a ghost.

Tara pulled Kyle to his feet and shuffled away from the noise. Peter came through the trees. His face had lost its color, and the angular cheeks seemed sunken. He still cradled May's body, and her slack face seemed strangely peaceful in the moonlight.

"Peter?" Tara waved for Kyle to stay behind her as she stepped forward. "Are you okay?"

He didn't answer. Slow, steady steps carried him toward the pier.

Tara cautiously followed. "What are you doing?"

"Giving May a place to rest," he grunted. "Anna's been lonely for a long time. She'll be happy to have family with her."

Tara stayed on the shore with Kyle by her side as they watched Peter. He followed the pier to its end then knelt on the last plank. The green-gray hands rose out of the lake, their fingers stretching toward Peter, and he lowered May into the arms. Together, they eased her body into the water.

Kyle hung on to the corner of Tara's jacket. She was glad to have his company. They watched Peter as he stared into the water, waiting for him to stand, but he never did. Instead, he swung his legs over the edge of the pier. Tara gasped and started forward. "Peter—"

He slid himself over the end of the dock and plunged into the lake. The motion, smooth and graceful, barely disturbed the water's surface.

"Stay here," Tara said. She jogged to the pier's end and knelt on the last plank, in the exact same space Peter had occupied seconds before, and looked down.

The water was inky black and impenetrable. A single bubble rose out of the depths and burst when it reached the surface, but otherwise, the water was undisturbed.

Tara sat back on her heels as a strange surreal sense of finality spread through her. She didn't know how to feel. Peter had killed, but he'd also shown her mercy. Now that both he and May were gone, relief mingled with a strange, deep grief that she couldn't explain. She stayed on the edge of the pier for several long minutes, until Kyle's hand patted the back of her shoulder.

"Let's go home," he said.

"Yeah."

CHAPTER 25
MORNING

THE WALK BACK TO the house felt like an eternity. The sky lightened by fractions, and by the time they exited the woods, sunlight framed the large, now seemingly mournful house.

For a moment, Tara considered never stepping back inside the building, but she knew that would be unreasonable. They were both tired and hungry, and getting to town wouldn't be an easy feat. Kyle obediently followed her onto the porch and through the door.

"What do you want for breakfast?" she asked.

"Not pancakes."

"I'll see if they have any cereal."

Kyle found spoons while Tara sorted through the cupboards. May had stocked the pantry with a dozen brands of cereal, none of them opened. She found the honey-flavored one Kyle liked and put it on the table in front of him. Then, on impulse, she turned on the kettle.

I could have a cup of tea and make him coffee. She nearly laughed at the idea of repeating the Folcrofts' daily habit—but the image hung with her as she retrieved the milk from the fridge and chose her own cereal.

We could actually do it. May said she left the house to us. We could stay here, just like they did, and look after each other. Kyle would take care of the garden. I would make our meals. There are enough cookbooks that I'm sure I could learn how to. We could uncover the house's secrets, find the war money they have hidden, and I can drive the Jeep into town whenever we need supplies. Even if people noticed May and Peter were missing, they probably wouldn't ask many questions.

Over time, we would become the new Folcrofts.

Tara sat opposite Kyle, unintentionally taking May's seat. He scooped huge spoonfuls of cereal into his mouth, his hand moving faster than his jaws could until his cheeks bulged with food.

If Mum's gone…this might be the closest thing to home we have.

"Whatcha thinking, Tara?" The words were garbled around his food.

She opened her mouth to tell him about the half-formed concept then caught herself. She laughed. "Just crazy thoughts."

"Please stop." He scrunched up his face. "I've had enough craziness to last me a lifetime."

She shook her head. "Yeah, me, too."

I'm not May. I'm Tara. I blog. I suck at geology. I hate hot weather and want to be a freelance journalist in a few years. We're not Folcrofts. And we're not staying in this cursed place.

She stood and moved around to the chair beside Kyle, where she normally sat. She poured some of Kyle's cereal, doused it in milk, and started eating.

"Do we have a plan?" Kyle asked.

"Sort of. I've got a few things to take care of before we leave. You can catch up on some sleep or finish a book or whatever while you wait."

"Sure."

She was surprised he didn't press her with more questions, but he seemed content to trust her. The pervasive fear that had dogged him since arriving at the house had finally fallen away, and he now kicked his feet and ate with gusto like he normally did. Tara smiled as she finished her own breakfast.

The idea of sleeping for a few hours was tempting, but she wanted to leave the Folcroft house as soon as she could. There was one thing she had to do before they could go, though.

While Kyle washed and put away their dishes, Tara climbed the stairs and followed the hallway. The locked room's door was still open, its handle falling out of the cracked wood, and Tara took a quick breath before stepping inside.

The scene looked wholly different in daylight. She could see the seats clearly, and the occupants were no longer drowning in shadows. There were four chairs: one for Harry Folcroft, one for Eileen Folcroft, and one for a smaller bundle, which must have been the young Christopher. The fourth chair was empty, but the indent in its cushion told Tara it was used frequently. She imagined May coming into the room every evening and sitting among her passed family. It made her shiver.

"Please forgive me," she said as she approached the nearest bundle. Long hair peeked out from under the blanket wrapping, identifying it as Eileen. Tara gingerly picked up the corners of the cloth and lifted. Eileen's body had long-since withered away, and her bones were light. Tara hefted the bundle and carried it out of the room, down the stairs, and through the front door.

The garden trenches she'd helped dig the day before were still open. They would be shallow graves, but Tara prayed it would be enough as she placed Eileen's body in the first indent.

She returned to the locked room. As she entered, she caught the faintest glimpse of a man pacing across the carpet before he vanished. She licked her lips then picked up Harry Folcroft. The room was quiet and empty during her third trip, when she retrieved Christopher. She lined the family up, one in each trench, then found the shovel leaned against the house's porch and began burying the Folcrofts.

The work was so absorbing that she didn't notice Kyle had followed until she heard the *chink* of a second shovel digging into the dirt. They worked side by side, piling the soft soil over the bundles to create burial mounds. Tara patted them down while Kyle disappeared around the house's corner. He returned carrying a large oval stone. He staggered under its weight, and Tara hurried to take one side of it. They placed the stone at the head of the first grave then made the trip two more times.

"Will that be enough?" Kyle asked.

They stood at the graves' feet and examined their work. Tara was breathing heavily and felt grimy but relieved. "I hope so. May believed their spirits didn't pass on because they hadn't been buried. I think this was why they asked for help."

"It's a nice place," Kyle said. "Close to the house but looking over the woods. The ground's rich enough that plants will grow over them in the next few years. I think I'd be happy to be buried like that."

"Me, too."

They bowed their heads and shared a moment of silence. Tara prayed that the Folcrofts would finally have peace and silently thanked them for saving her from the bunker. Then, wordlessly, the siblings returned inside.

Tara showered and changed while Kyle finished packing. Then, while he cleaned himself, she went down to the bunker and retrieved the key ring from where she'd left it in the metal door. The Jeep's key was easy to identify; it was newer and cleaner than the others. She unlocked the vehicle and helped Kyle load his things.

"Are we going to drive back home?" he asked.

"No. I can't drive well enough to cope with the highways. We'll take this as far as the town."

"Can I return the books to the library?"

Tara shrugged, so her brother raced back into the house and brought down an armful of his books. He loaded them next to the suitcases in the backseat, then they took the front, and Tara started the car.

She thanked her lucky stars the Jeep was an automatic. She let it crawl over the potholes and exposed roots lining the driveway then tried applying some power as they turned onto the main road. It was a nerve-wracking ride, and the car's side scraped the rock wall to their left twice, but Tara felt a surge of pride as they pulled into the town. Kyle only looked a little queasy and gave her a thumbs-up when she grinned at him.

Three empty parking spaces in a row gave her an easy target. The car's hood bumped the street sign in front of them, but Tara figured she would only cause more damage if she tried to correct the car's crooked angle. So she just turned it off.

Kyle undid his buckle. "Is it okay to leave it like this?"

"Yeah. We don't need it anymore, so I'll leave the keys in the ignition. If no one takes it, I guess it'll eventually be towed."

They carried Kyle's books back to the library. The woman behind the desk barely looked up as they dumped the piles onto her desk. Then they collected their luggage, returned to the street, and made their way to the bakery.

Pattie looked up as the bell over the door jingled, and surprise and pleasure lit her face. "Oh, hello, Tara. And you must be Kyle."

"Hey." There was no easy way to lead into her request, so Tara simply spread her hands and said, "You asked me the other day if I needed help. I'm ready to answer honestly. Yes. We need to get out of here. Can you drive us?"

"I—uh…Of course." Pattie, flustered, shot a look over her shoulder. "Um, Dave? Can you watch the shop for a bit?"

"It's a four-hour drive," Tara said and gave an apologetic smile.

"Sorry. But I'll make it up to you. You can have the Jeep parked in the street. And if you're curious, I can tell you the truth about the Folcroft family."

CHAPTER 26
HOME

TARA HAD NEVER LIKED hospitals. They were too white; the tile floors, the sheets, the walls, and the curtains competed to out-bright each other. The watercolor bird and nature scenes spaced sparingly along the hallway walls didn't do much to provide relief. There was one patch of color in the building that made Tara very happy, though.

Chris sat propped up in bed. One arm had to lay flat at her side for the drip line, but the other held Kyle's hand, her thumb running over his knuckles in soothing strokes.

"Are you sure you're happy at Mrs. Jennings's?"

Her voice was still raspy, though it was getting stronger each day. The doctors were talking about starting physiotherapy before the end of the week. She was eating more, too, and color was returning to her face.

Tara answered. "Yeah, she's been great. It's like a holiday. Kyle reads until he gets headaches, and I have a virtual monopoly over the computer."

Chris chuckled. "Don't fall too behind on your schoolwork. You won't be able to take much more time off."

"Don't worry; we'll be fine."

Kyle and Tara shared a brief glance. They'd been home for six days, and so far, the secret hadn't escaped.

Their mother thought they were staying at Mrs. Jennings's. Mrs. Jennings had been told they were with a nonexistent aunt. In reality, Kyle had gotten his wish: he and Tara stayed in their home. The shops were close enough for them to walk, and Tara had figured out how to pay bills with Chris's bank account. They caught the bus to the hospital each day.

She and Kyle worked together well. They shared the cleaning and the cooking, and only left the house when the neighbors weren't home to notice. The plan was to tell their mother about their stay at the Folcrofts' eventually, but not until she'd recovered enough to come home.

Tara had been dreaming about the stone house surrounded by woods. During idle afternoons, she found herself wondering if Peter's and May's ghosts lingered at the lake. She imagined walking through the meandering paths and listening to the birds and wild animals dart between the trees. If she stayed there long enough, she might eventually hear the shuffle of ghostly footsteps following just out of sight.

She knew she would return to the house eventually. Maybe after enough years had passed to soften the memories, she would drive up to the old stone building, walk through the creaking hallways, and visit the overgrown graves of the people she'd started to think of as her family.

CLOCKWORK

I HAD NEVER SEEN so many clocks in one place.

The room had no windows, just four walls with peeling varnish. The wooden floor had buckled and warped from water damage long ago. The door was narrow. So narrow that my guide and I had to turn our bodies sideways to slip inside.

I understood why the door was made that way now. It was to leave more of the wall free for clocks. They were everywhere, hung on countless black nails hammered into the wood, arranged on ornate tables, or, if they were large enough, standing free. The room should have felt cluttered, but the clocks had been positioned with care, meshed into an intricate display. I had the sensation that I'd stepped into a museum where every item was priceless.

"As you see, they have been neglected for too long."

My guide was old. His black suit had to be expensive, but the shoulders were warped from decades of hanging inside a closet. His thin gray hair had been combed neatly. Small glasses were placed over watery blue eyes. Everywhere, skin hung loose on his form; it drooped as jowls hung in flaps across his throat and creased over the backs of the bony hands he clasped ahead of himself.

I nodded, too overwhelmed to answer. My work normally involved repairing a single clock. Occasionally, if the customer was wealthy, I would be asked to check two or three in the one visit. I had never been presented with so many before.

"I…" My tongue stuck to the inside of my mouth. I tried to wet it. "Give me some time to check them, and I'll come up with a quote for you."

"I have no need for a quote." The hands unclasped, briefly, before returning to their original pose. "My offer is twenty thousand."

"Twenty—" I caught myself. That was an absurd number. Specialized knowledge carried a high price, but this was still beyond any amount I'd been imagining. When I looked across the clocks again, it was with mistrust. "It's really best if I know what I'm getting myself into before I start. I'll get you a quote, and hopefully, it will save you some money, as well."

"Money is not the issue. Rather, it is time." A chuckle came out, more like a wheeze than a laugh, and evaporated within two syllables. A joke about clocks. I wondered if that was what passed for humor in this house. "I wish for the work to begin immediately. And I am prepared to pay well for your compliance."

I took half a step back. There wasn't much room to move

without bumping into either my guide or one of the clocks. The door was closed. That hadn't felt threatening until that moment.

"If I may." One of the bony, wrinkled hands pressed against his chest. He bowed slightly, the jowls rocking as his head inclined. "Your hesitation is understandable. But I assure you, there is no attempt to cheat you here. If you are obligated to purchase any supplies, you will be reimbursed for those, as well. If the work cannot be done within a week, you will be released from the contract."

"A week?" My eyes flitted across the space. They landed on a second hand here, an hour hand there, a pendulum at my side. "I don't know if—"

"All I request is that you *try*." He smiled. It was a small motion, colorless lips lifting before drooping back to their neutral position. "I wish for my clocks to be repaired by next Saturday. If they are not, there is no penalty. You walk away with the full payment."

Four months' income for a week's work. It was too good to be true. I was seeing as many red flags as clocks.

His fingers rested on my arm. In any other situation, a client attempting to touch me was a signal to escape the house. But I didn't feel threatened in this case. The fingers were featherlight and undemanding. His voice cracked.

"These clocks are special to me. I used to care for them myself, but my eyesight is failing, and my fingers cannot feel the gears like they used to. I am not simply asking you to repair them. I am asking you to *care* about them."

Around me, the clocks shifted without moving. Hands turned, weights swung. I swallowed. "I can try."

"That is enough." The hand left my arm. He reached into the suit pocket and, a second later, pressed a check and a key into my palm. "Payment in advance. You may let yourself in and out of the house as you see fit. I will not always be about, and you do not need to announce your presence."

He turned toward the door. I stared at the key, my heart hammering, then called him to a halt as he touched the handle.

"What…uh, is there any particular work you want done on them?"

It was the most basic of questions, something I should have established at the beginning of the conversation. I felt foolish for not asking it earlier.

He didn't turn his body, but his head tilted a fraction, just far enough that I could see one drooping cheek. "Some run fast. Others run slow. They must all keep the same time. Down to the second."

With that, he slipped through the narrow door. The latch clicked as it shut behind him. I turned back to face the clocks. Alone with them, I could hear the ticking. The sound ran wild, each second hand creating its own beat, until they bled into something close to a ragged hum.

I took a breath to brace myself, placed my toolkit on the floor at my side, and tucked the key and payment into my pocket. It seemed wise to know exactly what I was facing as soon as possible, so I walked around the room, giving each clock a second of attention.

They were an eclectic collection and, as far as I could tell, all antique. Most were made of wood. A handful were metal. Four were made entirely of stone—a rare choice. And, strangest of all, a couple seemed to have been upholstered with leather.

Some were small enough to fit into my palm, just barely large enough to hold the dial and a keyhole to wind them up. The largest was a grandfather clock that nearly reached the ceiling; I would have to stretch onto my toes to touch its top. Some were plain, with smooth surfaces and simple designs. Others were made of complex, interwoven carvings that seemed designed to trap dust.

I had to start somewhere. I picked what looked like an easy target—a carriage clock the size of my head that had been resting on one of the three tables. I glanced behind myself to ensure the door was still shut, then I sat cross-legged on the floor with the clock resting in my lap as I opened it and explored its insides.

In the age of digital clocks and battery-run quartz movements, it was easy to underestimate how complex a mechanical clock was. They were full of gears, weights, levers, and springs, nestled together, each relying on the others to do their job. Little disks of teeth, constantly chewing but never swallowing. They were expected to turn their whole lives, with only the twist of a key once a week to keep them moving.

The first clock held all of the trappings I had expected. Fragments of dust had accumulated, and two of the gears were showing early signs of rust. I took out one of the tiny plastic cups from my kit and filled it with solution. I plucked the gears out one by one, dropping them into the cup, saving them from the gnawing effects of age.

The gears sat in the treatment while I used compressed air and cotton buds to clean accumulated grime out of the body. Old, dried oil came off in black streaks. The clocks' owner had requested that I care for them like he would, so I did, giving every corner of the machine attention until it was impeccable. Then I began to refit the mechanics, winding the hair-thin spring to the perfect tension, and used light dabs of oil to make sure every part moved with smooth precision.

I breathed deeply as I closed the door and wound the clock. My guide had asked for to-the-second accuracy. I used my digital clock, which was programmed to UTC, to set the wooden creature's time. I watched it, making sure it would not slip out of its tempo, ensuring it was not slow. Once I was satisfied, I placed it back on the table.

Each clock had a unique session. Some were struggling with rust. For others, the balance wheel was stiff. For still others, the gear trains had come loose. My miniature screwdrivers and needle-nose pliers dipped in and out of the clocks like feasting birds.

I didn't leave the room until the gnawing in my stomach was impossible to ignore. As I stepped outside, I looked up at the sky and saw it was covered with stars.

Night had arrived unexpectedly early. It had been easy to lose myself in the job. The tiny gears and thin little metal hands had absorbed my focus.

That night, I lay awake in bed, thinking of the clocks. I didn't sleep well and woke while it was still dark. I was back at the room shortly after dawn, using my key to let myself in.

It was a relief to be back among the ticking hands. The gears felt familiar between my fingers. Scratched glass dials could be polished to smoothness. Dull wood was restored. I removed jams from around pendulums, checking balances and counter-balances, watching the weights dance.

None of the clocks were marked, I realized. Antiques weren't manufactured as aggressively as mass-market products, but each clock worker would tend to hold to a style through his life. Tall and thin or rounded. Hands always with a particular shape. Horologists learned to recognize them like old friends. A signature, not unlike an artist's, was often engraved or stamped somewhere on the timepiece.

These clocks had all been handmade, that was clear, but none of their makers had left a name. As I moved through the room, I became more entranced by the idea. I was surrounded by custom clocks, some requiring a hundred hours to construct, but no signatures.

I began to wonder if my host might have been the builder. He clearly cared for them. They could have been his life's work, a business that had never been about making money.

A wild idea ran through my mind. Would he let me build a clock for his collection? I'd never taken on the task before. No one wanted to spend thousands on a handmade clock unless the maker was famous. My work was all about restoring antiques. I tended to the works of old masters, never creating any of my own.

The idea captivated me. I wanted my creation held in this room among so many other beautiful examples. It would never be seen by anyone else, most likely. But, somehow, that made it even more alluring. But I hadn't been hired to build a clock. My job was to restore. I put my head back down and returned my focus to the lever I was cleaning.

As my work progressed, a tempo began to rise out of the droning. My clocks, timed down to a fraction of a second, were running in perfect synchrony. Their beat rose above the others, and with each new clock, it grew louder.

I picked up one of the leather-bound creations. After so much wood, it was a nice change to feel the smooth material under my fingers. The clock wasn't large, but it had a window for its pendulum and a little handle for the door. I opened it and pointed my flashlight inside. The pendulum was made out of a strange material. I thought it might be stone, but it wasn't cold or dense enough. It had been carved like stone, though. Interwoven lines ran through the off-white material, and I began to suspect I was looking at driftwood. An odd choice in an odd clock.

The machine had been built with care. Every angle and nook aligned perfectly. As I worked on the clock, my chest began to burn, and I realized I'd forgotten to breathe.

Like the day before, I didn't leave until exhaustion and hunger drove me out. I hated that my body was too feeble to continue the work. As I walked through the front door, the ticking beat followed me, running like a drum, matching my heart.

At home, I felt feverish. My fingers shook as I forced spoonfuls of dry cereal into my mouth. My bed, normally so alluring, seemed repulsive. Did I even have the right to rest while the clocks were still out of time?

Sleep was sweaty and brief. I didn't even wait for dawn. I jogged to the house through the dead of night, the recipient of scarcely four hours of rest but more awake than I'd ever felt. My breath misted, but I didn't feel the cold.

None of the house's windows had light in them, but I didn't have any qualms about unlocking the door and stepping inside. My guide hadn't disturbed me before, and I didn't expect him to that night, either.

A groan escaped as I sank to my knees among the clocks. I'd spread a cloth over the wooden floor, and it held endless gears and springs in stages of repair. I was grateful to be back.

The day passed too quickly. I became angry when I was forced to put down my work in order to drink or eat. My eyes ached, and my head throbbed, but I welcomed the pain. It was a sign that I was doing a good job. The ticking was growing louder.

More clocks passed under my hands. Metal, stone, leather, glass. No substance had been neglected in the collection. I started to work on multiple clocks at once, unwilling to leave my hands empty if gears had to soak or their speed needed to be timed. It should have been chaos, but it was beautiful synchrony. The clocks told me what they needed. All I had to do was listen and obey.

There were no windows in the room to let in natural light or to warn me of passing time. I didn't even realize how long I'd spent there until, while setting one clock's time, I saw the day displayed in tiny print on my digital control. Thursday.

I didn't remember going home the previous night or the night before that. I must have, I guessed. I couldn't have been standing otherwise. A quiet voice whispered that I should probably leave then. Get some sleep and some food. Step back from the clocks. But as I looked up at the walls, the idea faded.

My work was nearly done. Their voices rang out, clear and sharp, ticking in unison. Only a few still needed attention. And I wasn't tired. I could keep going.

Those last clocks were restored in a feverish panic. One moment, I was desperate to be done and escape the room. The next, I dreaded leaving. But, no matter what I felt, it was all painted with a tinge of alarm. I was facing the end. Like facing a train as it ran toward me. Whether I longed for it or hated it, I couldn't escape.

My hands shook miserably as I returned the gears to the final clock. My heart hurt, and my eyes burned. I set the time, getting it perfect, down to a fraction of a second, to match the others. Then I placed it onto the table and listened.

They ticked together, but they were not perfect.

I moaned, a sick feeling rising inside. My fingers dug through my hair, and I instantly regretted it as my hands came away covered in oil. I couldn't contaminate these clocks with my slick flesh. I stepped outside and washed urgently, furiously, my mind fixating on the ticking.

It wasn't perfect. Not yet. The second hands all moved nearly at once, but some came in early, and some came in late. It created a dulled effect to the noise. Muffled. Not sharp and clear the way it was supposed to be.

I moved through the room, bending close to each clock, listening to see where it fell. I found one that was too soon, took it down, and reset the time.

Not quite. Again. Not quite. *Again.*

Why was I so broken that I couldn't get it right?

Again. My hands shook. Again.

I bit my lip until it bled. Again. I clicked my tongue, and suddenly, the time was right.

The clock matched the tempo perfectly. It wasn't a fraction of a second off. It was narrowed down to a hundredth, maybe even a thousandth, of a second. I placed it back on the shelf, breathing deeply.

There were so many other clocks that needed further tuning. But that was all right. I still had time. It was only Thursday.

I clicked my tongue to find the time. It worked better than trying to match it to the digital reader, which I left discarded by my case. I'd internalized the count. All I had to do was click my tongue in time, and my fingers followed, setting the beat perfectly.

A new frustration rose. As I worked, some of the older clocks began to slip out of time. Not by much. But enough. I had to tear them back open, going through the mechanisms again, getting them even, getting them perfect. I didn't resent the clocks. I resented the fallible human skin that was falling down around me.

My tongue grew numb from clicking, but it didn't lose its

beat. I let it go constantly, even when I was realigning gears. It soothed me, quieted the panic in my mind.

I reached for a tool in one of my pockets and found a piece of paper instead. I took it out. A check. *The* check. My mouth twisted; the little slip of paper felt dirty. He expected me to do this for *money*. I crumpled the check and threw it toward the door.

It was Saturday. I didn't need to check my digital clock to be sure. I knew it in my bones; each click counted a second; each second meted out a fraction of an hour. I wasn't a slave to time any longer. Time was inside me. We counted up to midnight together, neither rushing nor panicking. We knew how long we had, and we knew how long we needed for the work.

The pendulums swung smoothly. The wood was polished. The glass was clear. I placed the final clock back onto its table and knelt in the center of the floor.

Tick. Click. Tick. Click.

We were perfect. Not a single clock was out of beat. They rang sharp, aligned, magnificent, the way they were supposed to be. I sang with them, matching them, grateful that I could be a part of them.

The door opened at midnight. My guide stepped inside. He carried a small wooden box. His skin drooped, loose at every angle, as it had on that first night a week ago. He smiled. It wasn't a thin, sad expression this time. It was pleased. "You did a fine job."

I knew I had. They were perfect.

He knelt beside me and placed the box ahead of himself. All

of his movements were steady and measured. He had made the clocks; I was certain of it by that point.

I lay on the floor. My eyes were half-blind. My hands were red where the skin had been ground down. I clicked my tongue in beat.

A week ago, when I'd taken the job, my guide had said there would be no penalty if I didn't finish the work. At the time, I hadn't understood what he was telling me: that there *was* a penalty if I did.

He opened the box. The scalpel came out. I didn't feel it, though I felt parts of myself being removed. Bones, mostly. Flaps of skin. I was grateful he left my tongue alone, so that I could still keep time.

Those parts of myself were washed. Dried. Treated. Washed again. And then he began the carving. I was to be intricate, he told me. I was not a simple person, so my creation should not be either. My femurs became the back of the clock. My ribs helped build the cavity where the gears were kept. A disk from my spine, filed down and fused with metal, was weighted for the pendulum. My skull created form for the dial, and my finger bones were whittled down into second and hour hands.

I had never felt a human bone before. When I'd opened the leather-bound clocks, I'd thought it felt like driftwood. I wanted to laugh at myself. I couldn't. Not without losing the timing.

My skin was tanned into leather. It covered the structural bones, hiding the gaps between them and protecting the delicate gears inside. He was a master. Every angle was clean. All of my lines were straight. No one except he and I could have guessed the clock's origin.

He set my time and checked my speed. I was perfect. He smiled. Then he carefully, lovingly arranged me on one of the tables, between the clocks I had doted on. He stepped through the door. It closed behind him. I kept time.

AUTHOR'S NOTE

I'm in love with Australia's Blue Mountains. A single main road runs along the mountain ridge, with towns sprouting off each side like ribs. The area has a very strong lean toward alternative and natural living; small, esoteric businesses abound, and cafés serve produce from the owners' gardens.

The Blue Mountains are also known for the secondhand stores. Dozens of them are scattered through different towns; some tiny, some multistory, all crowded with dusty shelves and endless curiosities.

I was browsing one of those stores when I found myself in an alcove filled with clocks. The three walls around me were covered with them, all ticking, the beats all out of sync. It was beyond unsettling, and I couldn't endure more than a few seconds before hurrying back to safer ground. I did my best to capture that uneasy, slightly surreal sensation in this story. I hope it leaves you as uncomfortable as that clock-filled alcove left me.

SUB BASEMENT

"IT'S YOUR TURN," ANDREW said as he dropped a sheet of paper onto my desk.

I glanced over the list of names and cursed under my breath. There had to be at least twenty of them. "I could have sworn it was Carlie's turn next."

Andrew gave me a lopsided grin. "Nope, she did the archive run last week. It's tax time, man. Everyone wants their records dug up. You know that."

I glanced around and saw that the half-dozen employees within hearing distance had stopped their work to listen in on the conversation. Most of them had the decency to swivel back to their computers when I made eye contact, but Tyson, the office joker, took the opportunity to pull out his tie and hold it taut above his head like a noose. I hated Tyson.

"You know how it works," Andrew said. "Take a flashlight and a jacket, and work fast. There're only twenty-two names here. It shouldn't take you more than half an hour. You'll be done before you know it."

I grudgingly took the list and headed for the lift.

Everyone hated getting the archive run. It was a trip into the very bottom level of the high-rise to retrieve—or return—files of customers who no longer did business with us. Normally, the visits were infrequent—once every three or four weeks—but over the last month, we'd been inundated with customers wanting details of their canceled accounts so they could submit tax returns.

I'd only done one archive run before, eight months previously, for two folders, and I had no interest in repeating the experience.

The archive's level wasn't listed on the building's floor plans, but most people called it the Sub Basement. It was permanently dark, icy cold, and smelled like rotting paper and plants. Many rumors circulated about the neglected level. Most were probably hyperbolic, but enough had a ring of truth to them to make the Sub Basement a favorite gossip point in the office.

I got into an empty lift and selected the blank button at the bottom of the panel. The carriage held still for a second before beginning its descent. I wiped my sweating palms on my pants and loosened my tie.

"It's no big deal," I told myself. Dozens of people had made the run without seeing anything out of the ordinary. And even when…well, Joan had suffered from a heart condition, anyway.

The display above the elevator's door listed the levels we were passing. I worked near the top of the building, on the eighteenth floor. The numbers descended until they read 0—the first basement—then 00—the second basement. The display froze on 00 while the carriage continued to descend into the Sub Basement.

The elevator stopped with a jolt, and the doors slid open. Outside was a long corridor. I could only see as far as the elevator's light penetrated. Beyond that was ink black.

I stepped out and reached to the right. A row of flashlights and waterproof jackets hung from hooks on the concrete wall. I took one of each and turned my light on as the elevator's doors closed.

The Sub Basement's lights had failed four years ago, leaving it in permanent darkness. Management had hired electricians, but the lights couldn't be repaired without drilling into the concrete supports and compromising the stability of the building. Management had promised to put up temporary lights, but somehow, they never made it into the budget.

I flicked my flashlight beam across the walls of the corridor. The concrete was discolored from a steady seepage of water. Carts, the kind used in libraries, stood against the walls. Most were broken. Rust had stained many of them red. Twenty-two folders would be a large armful, but not enough to make me search for a working cart. I hurried past them.

The double door at the end of the hallway used a push handle to open. I pressed on it, but it stuck. I grimaced and rose onto my toes, putting my full weight on the handle, until it scraped down and opened the doors.

The stories about the Sub Basement were copious and of dubious veracity. Paul from IT told anyone who would listen that it was never supposed to be built, but the construction crew made a mistake when reading the plans. I thought Paul was full of it.

Preeta had said she saw rats the size of small dogs when she was on an archive run. I'm a little more inclined to believe her—she tends to be honest.

The worst were the stories about the five employees who'd quit, each after going on an archive run. Supposedly, they'd asked for their unpaid salary to be mailed to them then walked straight out of the building, not even stopping long enough to clean out their desks or say goodbye.

I'd thought the stories were fiction—until I witnessed it myself. The most recent quitter was Riley, who had worked opposite me. He was a quiet guy, but we'd gotten along well. I'd always thought he was reliable. Steady. Then one afternoon, he went on an archive run and didn't come back. HR told us he had quit. They cleaned out his desk overnight. The rumor mill had a field day.

I moved my flashlight about the Sub Basement, squinting to pick out shapes in the dancing light. To the left were filing boxes stacked nearly to the ceiling. Immediately in front of me and to the right were shelves—nearly a hundred of them—with thousands upon thousands of files.

The air was incredibly cold. I held the flashlight with my teeth and tucked the paper between my knees before slipping into the waterproof jacket. It wouldn't provide much warmth, but at least it would protect me from the drips.

The room was about the size of a football field. Most of the files had been accumulated before the company went digital five years previously, and HR didn't have any motivation—or room—to move them to a higher, warmer level. I suspect HR would have found plenty of motivation if they were the ones responsible for archive runs.

The files were divided into three sections—one for each decade the company had been operating—and each decade was arranged alphabetically according to the customer's surname.

My list had the decades handwritten next to the names, and was arranged from most recent to oldest. First up were eight names from the last decade, which would be found in the boxes to the left of the door.

The universal advice was to get in and out of Sub Basement quickly. The more time people spent there, the wilder their tales became.

Jerome said he believes there's a gas leak with hallucinogenic properties. He has warned every new employee not to light up in the Sub Basement in case it triggered an explosion.

I couldn't smell anything, but that didn't mean he wasn't right.

The first file—ANDERSON, Patricia—was easy to find, and I pulled it out of its box. Something rattled from farther in the room. I froze, listening hard.

Silence.

I exhaled through my teeth and started scanning the names again.

Gregory thought bats had infested the Sub Basement. He'd supposedly found a nest of them in the corner of the room, but they were blind and deformed, and they'd screamed at him when he got too close.

I found the second and third names together and tugged them both out. I set my small pile on the ground and went to work looking for the fourth name.

Something brushed my ankle, and I jumped back, bumping into the shelves behind me and nearly knocking them over. The flashlight's beam was jittery as I angled it at the ground, but I felt a buzz of relief when I saw the strip of plastic wrap poking out from under the boxes. I must have grazed it.

I moved forward again to continue my search and felt something prickly stick into my neck. I swiped at it. The sensation clung to my hand as I pulled it away and angled my flashlight at it.

A glossy black insect hung on my fingers. It was large and flat, and its body was segmented like a wasp's. Its six legs had hooks that dug into my skin, and large mandibles protruded from its oblong face.

I let out a choked cry of disgust and tried to flick the insect off, but it dug its spiked legs in harder, piercing my skin. Desperate, I slapped the back of my hand against the bookcase, hoping to crush the creature. Its body convulsed on impact, and it dropped to the ground then scuttled under the shelf.

I drew in shallow, ragged breaths as I moved away and brought the flashlight up to examine my hand. The cuts were small, but they stung.

Something on my arm moved at the same time as I became

aware of many small objects hanging onto my back. I froze then carefully turned the light toward my arm. One of the insects, larger than the first, clung to my elbow. Further up, another one had latched onto my shoulder.

The flashlight made a dull metallic noise as I dropped it on the concrete ground. I hardly dared breathe as I moved my hands to undo the waterproof jacket's buttons.

Two of the insects shifted on my back. I squinted my eyes closed as my skin crawled and goose bumps rose on my arms. I undid the final button and, in a smooth motion, shrugged out of the jacket, skidded away from it, and scooped up the flashlight and paper at the same time.

I turned the light on the plastic jacket. Two of the insects burrowed into the cloth to hide. I let my breath out and shuddered then ran my hands over my hair, my neck, and my legs to check that I was clear.

They must have fallen on me when I bumped into the shelf. I'd never seen insects that big. *What were they? Wasps? Some sort of cockroach?*

"Work fast," I reminded myself. "Get the folders and leave."

I left the jacket on the ground and went back to my search, being careful not to touch shelves I didn't need to.

The fourth name was hard to find, but the fifth came easily. I took my stack of folders back to the doorway and left them on a dry bit of concrete. No point carrying them about with me.

The next folder I needed was on the other side of the temporary cardboard filing cases. As I rounded the corner, I saw a kitchen and break room indented into the wall. Next to them was a door leading to the bathroom. Each floor, including the Sub Basement, had its own amenities.

Hanna loved to tell the story of how she'd needed to use the bathroom while on an archive run. The details seemed to get embellished with each retelling, but she did have the cuts on her legs to show for it.

I made quick work of the next three folders and put them on the stack next to the door. The fourth one was misfiled, and I had to crouch to search for it. Something cold and wet landed on the back of my neck, and I jerked back, frightened the insects had returned.

It was some sort of slime. I scraped it off the back of my neck to examine it. It was clear and thicker than water, but not quite jelly, like dense saliva, only icy cold.

I thought I heard rattling above me and pointed my flashlight toward the ceiling. Like the ground and walls, it was discolored, but I didn't see anything that could account for the drips. The slimy sensation on my hands made me feel nauseous. I didn't want to wipe it on my pants, and there was nowhere else I could clean myself—except the bathroom.

"Damn," I whispered. "Damn, damn, damn."

I nudged the door open and took a moment to shine my light over the insides. It was very similar to the bathrooms on the higher floors. Directly in front of me were three sinks, each with their own soap pump. At the back of the room was a paper towel dispenser. To the right were four stalls with tall, dark-gray doors, all closed. The walls and floor were tile, while the ceiling was the same concrete as the rest of the floor.

Unlike the higher levels, the Sub Basement's bathroom was falling apart. Many of the tiles were cracked, and fungus and mold grew in the crevices. Dark stains ran down the sink bowls, toward the drains. The bin was overflowing with decaying paper towels, and the glass mirror above the sinks was clouded with age, showing a blurred imitation of the stalls behind it.

I placed my flashlight on the corner of one of the sinks. It reflected off the tiles, providing modest illumination for the room.

I went to the paper towels first, intending to blot off the ooze. The front of the dispenser was cracked open, as though something large had been rammed into it, and towels spilled out of the top. I pulled at one of them, but it fell apart between my fingers.

The air was too damp; moisture had gotten into the towels and rotted them during the five years the Sub Basement had been unoccupied. I grimaced and turned to the taps. I chose the sink with the least discoloration and turned the tap on. Grinding and shuddering rose from under the tiles at my feet, and I jumped back. The whole room sounded alive at that moment, filled with echoes of noise as long-unused pipes were forced to carry water.

Dark-red liquid spat out of the tap, splashing over the edge of the sink as it burst out of its pipes.

"It's just rust," I told myself, trying to slow my heart rate. "Nothing to be frightened of."

The red water flowed for nearly a minute before it became

clear. I waited until there was no trace of discoloration then dunked my slime-coated hand under the flow. The water must have been near freezing; my skin smarted wherever it touched, and I pulled my hand away as soon as it was clean.

I glanced into the mirror and jolted back. One of the stall doors stood wide open. I could have sworn they were all closed when I'd come into the bathroom, but it stood ajar, exposing a broken toilet inside.

The pipes below me increased their noise to a scream, and the water flowing from the tap reduced to a trickle then began to spew something thick and inky black into the sink.

I turned off the tap, but the liquid kept coming. It poured out in globs that contained something strangely brittle, like decayed plant matter, and painted the sink black. An oily, metallic smell rose from it, making me gag, and stuck in my nose even when I held my breath.

The gunk was too thick to drain quickly. The sink filled and began to overflow, and I stepped back to avoid the splatter. The pipes below my feet wailed and screeched, then abruptly, they fell silent. The thick black flow reduced to a drip.

I glanced around the room.

All four stall doors were open.

I grabbed my light and left the room—not quite running, but not loitering, either.

Once I'd put a dozen paces between myself and the bathroom, I stopped and rubbed at my eyes with my spare hand. It was shaking.

Finish the job quickly. Ignore any distractions. Ten more minutes, and you'll be out of here.

I found the misfiled folder and put it on the stack by the door. I examined the list and found that I'd finished with the most recent section. The next batch of files would be in the tall wooden shelves.

My task became more difficult then. The boxes had been filed alphabetically, but the shelves only collected the first letters together, forcing me to flip through whole bundles to find the correct name. Frustration built in my stomach. I had fourteen names left—there was no way I would finish quickly.

The Sub Basement was freezing. My breath clouded in front of my face as I muttered names to myself. Occasionally, I thought I heard words being muttered back at me from across the room, but whenever I stopped to listen, it fell silent.

Jenna had said she'd heard people talking to her. The voices sounded like old men, and when she'd gone searching for the source, she'd found letters scratched into one of the walls. Other employees said they'd looked for the scratchings but hadn't been able to find them.

The stack of files by the door grew slowly. By the time I'd found the second-to-last name, I must have been in the Sub Basement for nearly an hour.

I was breathing hard from the repetitive crouching and stretching and shivering from the cold—but I only had one name left: PERRICK, Clarissa.

She was in a category of her own—the 60s to 70s decade.

Why she would want her records more than forty years after she'd done business with us was beyond me.

I paced up and down the shelves as I looked for her section, but the records seemed to go back only as far as 1970. *Did Andrew make a mistake on the decade beside her name?*

Then I found the door hidden at the back of the room. It was tall and metal, with a push lever on the front, just like at the entrance to the Sub Basement. A faded plaque at the top read *Archives 1960–1970.*

"Hell," I whispered.

I dropped the four files onto the stack I'd collected at the entrance to the Sub Basement. I was tempted to return to the office without the last folder and claim I couldn't find it, but I knew management would be ruthless. Clarissa Perrick wanted her records, so she was going to get her records one way or another. They would either send me back down or send someone in my place—and that was a fast way to become unpopular in the office.

I returned to the door, rubbed my hands across my face, then pressed down on the lever. The door ground open, its hinges wailing, and brilliantly cold air blew through the gap.

I held the flashlight in front of myself as I crept through the doorway. My ears suddenly filled with the clang of my shoes on metal as the concrete flooring ended. Beyond the door was a staircase—not one of the solid, enclosed concrete ones, but a rusted metal fixture that had been screwed onto the wall. I pointed my flashlight over the railing, but the light wasn't strong enough to bring the floor below into relief. All I could make out were some shelves and what looked like a lounge area.

"Damn it," I whispered. "A basement below the Sub Basement." No one from the office had said anything about another level.

I moved with intense caution, brushing one hand against the wall to my left and swinging the flashlight across the steps in front of my feet. Ten steps down, the railing to my right disappeared. Where it ended was bent, as though someone had torn off a section. I moved closer to the wall.

Another five steps, and I nearly slipped. The metal slats had been dry up to that point, but some type of slime, unnervingly similar to what had dripped onto the back of my neck, coated the rest. I slowed down even more, placing each foot with painstaking care. A little farther on, the slime developed on the wall. It felt strangely warm under my fingers, and I recoiled in disgust. I became aware of the stench of organic decay. The farther down the stairs I went, the stronger it became until it felt as if it were coating my tongue.

I reached the concrete floor and stopped to catch my breath. My fingers were shaking as I loosened my tie to allow for easier breathing. The room wasn't as large as the floor above had been, but it was deep. I angled my light up the stairs and could barely make out the top. I turned slowly, bringing shapes into focus with the narrow beam of my flashlight, and gazed into the room with sick fascination.

Shelves, much like in the room above, stood in two straight rows through the center of the room. Two of the closer ones had fallen over like dominoes, the first propped up by a couch. Folders and pieces of paper had fallen out of it and were scattered across the floor.

I turned my flashlight over the mess. Many of the files had rotted in the dampness, but the ones toward the top were still mostly intact. Typewritten titles such as "Case 2461" and "Case 9330" were displayed on the front. I nudged one of the folders open with my shoe and instantly recoiled.

Inside was a black-and-white photograph of a disfigured man. He was missing both eyes, and where his nose should have been was a black hole. An open mouth showed badly deformed teeth. To either side of him, two doctors—passive, expressionless, and dressed in white lab coats—held the man still with a hand on each of his arms.

I shuddered as I turned away.

To the left of the shelves were couches. I skipped my light over them in morbid fascination. They were badly decayed, sagging and rotting—probably the cause of the stench.

Several had large stains on them. The discoloration was spread across the backrest and concentrated on the cushions below, almost as if…

No, I told myself. *No, not as if people had been left to rot in the seats. That's a dangerous way to be thinking. Find the folder, and get out.*

I moved between the shelves, looking for the familiar customer folder markings, but they were all numbers. "Case 0058," "Case 4902." No names.

"Damn it, where are you, Clarissa?"

I panned my flashlight across the walls, looking for any bookcases or filing cabinets I might have missed. Paintings had been glued to the wall opposite me, creating a haphazard patchwork of color. They depicted strange faces and distorted shapes.

I was close to giving up when my light passed over a door at the back of the room. Bronze signs were posted above it.

RESPITE ROOMS

PHARMACY

CONDITIONING ROOMS

BRIGHTWATER ACCOUNTANTS—ARCHIVE

I chewed on the inside of my cheek. I'd thought the whole building belonged to Brightwater. *Maybe another business worked in the basement levels at one time.*

Perhaps the company's owner, Paul Brightwater, had rented the basement when he started his business then bought the entire building later on. That would explain why the file for Clarissa Perrick, one of Brightwater's first customers, was squirreled away in the nightmarish sub-sub-basement.

I glanced back at the numbered files and the rotting couches then pushed through the metal door. A long corridor with multiple doors stretched in front of me. I moved carefully, swinging my light to check the plaques above each side-shoot. The doors were old, many of the hinges were rusted, and the glass panes set in the front were blurry from accumulated dust and grease.

I peered through the window of the first door I passed, labeled *Respite Rooms*. Beyond it was another long hallway with many doors of its own. Medical trays were left abandoned along the walls. The window was too blurry to offer a clear view, but I thought I glimpsed movement near the back of the hallway. I paused, holding my flashlight still, but I couldn't see anything else.

My curiosity wasn't strong enough to make me linger, so I quickened my pace as I passed the other passageways. *Brightwater Accountants* was the last door to the left. I paused in the entryway and moved my flashlight over the room. It was a small office with a bare, defunct bulb hanging from the ceiling and age stains across the walls. A cheap desk sat to one side with two broken chairs opposite it. Behind the desk was a filing cabinet, which I hurried to and opened eagerly.

"Come on, Clarissa Perrick, where are you?" I muttered to myself. I checked under P and felt sick when I found only four files there, none of them belonging to Clarissa.

I'd come too far to turn back empty-handed. I checked under C, in case she had accidentally been filed under her first name. When I didn't find her there, I began to rifle through the other folders, desperate and frustrated.

She wasn't there. I slammed the drawer closed in a fit of anger and froze as the slamming noise echoed back at me from the hallway. I moved to the office door and shone my light down the length of the hallway. It was empty, but the door at the end was closed.

My breath whistled as I let it out through clenched teeth and began jogging for the door. *To hell with Brightwater and their missing files. They'll have to do without.*

I pushed the door's handle to open it. It stuck in place. I pushed harder, then pulled, jiggled the handle, and pressed my entire weight on it.

It didn't budge. I'd been locked in.

My flashlight beam jittered over the walls as I turned and looked down the hallway. *Had the door locked itself, like they did in some hospitals? Was there a button to open it again?*

No, no button. I found only stained concrete walls, stained concrete floor, and blank metal doors with fogged glass.

I knelt beside the door and tried to slow my breathing while I thought. They'll come looking for me if I'm down here for too long. *Just like they'd searched for Joan...*

I cringed and pressed my sweating palms against my eyelids. I would never forget the moment they brought Joan out of the Sub Basement. Nearly everyone from my floor had stayed late as we waited for news. We'd congregated outside the lifts, talking in hushed voices as police and emergency workers swarmed through the building.

The lights above the only elevator that went to the Sub Basement lit up. We pushed forward, eager to see Joan, ask her what had gone wrong, and possibly hear a new tale of the macabre firsthand. But the elevator doors opened, and all that came out were four rescue workers and a sheet-covered body on a gurney.

She'd had heart problems, I reminded myself. *You're young and fit, and they'll find you.*

Eventually.

I stood up. There was another option. Health and Safety codes meant that every building above a certain size had to have two exits for each floor. There was another way out.

I started down the hallway. The room at the end, Brightwater's office, was a dead end. So was the pharmacy, which was missing its door. I glanced inside but didn't linger—every drawer and cupboard was open and empty.

The door to the conditioning rooms was locked. That left the respite rooms.

The handle creaked when I pressed on it, but it opened, granting me access to the long hallway of abandoned medical carts and closed doors.

I shined my light at the first door to my left. Through the blurred glass, I was able to make out a metal examination table. Leather straps were draped over its dulled surface, and the concrete floor was stained.

The following four doors all led to bedrooms. They had identical accommodations: plain, rusted metal bed frames held mattresses in varying stages of decay. A chair and a bedpan sat neatly against the walls. A single hand-painted sheet of paper hung above each of the beds—two had nature scenes, one was abstract splotches of color, and one depicted a face with no eyes.

The hallway turned a corner. As I walked, I became aware of a noise behind me. It sounded almost like shuffling, stuttering steps on the concrete floor. I froze. As though it were a switch being turned, the noise stopped.

An echo? I held my breath and scuffed my shoe across the ground. It made a dull thumping noise. No echo.

I started walking again. The noise was gone, but a horrible feeling of dread had taken its place. I walked faster and faster, and the flashlight's beam jittered erratically in front of me as I broke into a sprint. I didn't bother stopping to look into the rooms I passed—I just wanted to get out of there.

I rounded another corner, and the hallway ended in a double door, just like the entryway to the Sub Basement. Sweat trickled down the back of my neck even as the icy air coaxed plumes of condensation out of my breath. I was shivering almost too severely to keep the light steady as I pressed my face against the cold metal door and peered through the glass window.

It was too blurred for me to see anything. I flexed my shoulders, took a deep breath, and pushed the handle down. The door opened, and I could have laughed from relief. A landing stretched for a few feet ahead of me. Beyond that, stairs led upward.

Then I raised my flashlight and saw the rubble.

There had been a cave-in, probably a long time ago, from how settled it looked. Slabs of concrete, natural rock, bricks, and dirt mingled in a pile partway up the stairs, effectively blocking the exit.

I ran my hand over my mouth. *I might still be able to dig my way through. If the rubble isn't too deep, I could shift enough to get past it, get back to the Sub Basement, take the lift up to the twenty-second floor, and hand in my resignation, just like all of the other souls who quit after doing an archive run.*

The entire area was smothered in thick dust. I shrugged out of my jacket and tried to find somewhere clean to hang it. Eventually, I slung it over a metal support that stuck out from the broken wall.

I began climbing the rubble, moving slowly and testing each foothold to make sure it was solid. I hadn't gone more than a few steps when I noticed something strange—other footprints marred the dust. They were fainter than mine and belonged to smaller shoes. Someone had been there before me.

I crouched down to get a closer look at the print. I guessed it belonged to a woman's shoe, and, although it had left a clear imprint in the half-inch-thick layer of grime, fresh sheets of dust softened its appearance. It was old.

Maybe the owner of this print had been faced by the same obstacle I was but had gotten through? I followed the tracks up the collapsed stairwell, turning my light backward and forward over the debris to follow the progress of the scuffed footprints and occasional smudge from where a hand had been used.

Near the top of the pile, the tracks stopped. I looked for a gap in the debris and held up my hand to feel for a breeze, but the way was clearly blocked. I sat down on a slab of concrete and evaluated my situation.

To my right, a strange shape leaned against the wall. I jerked backward in shock and turned my flashlight toward it.

Coiled up in the corner, leaning against the wall and holding a folder tightly to its chest, was a human body. At first, I thought it was a skeleton, but it still had skin, dried and stretched tight across the bones after months of exposure to the icy air. Its eye sockets were empty, and its mouth was open, exposing a shriveled tongue and discolored teeth. Dirty blonde hair lay in limp coils on its shoulders. I looked more closely at its clothes, and a horrible sick feeling surged through me as I recognized our office uniform.

The clue to the body's identity was the shoes: leather, with red buckles. Only one person in the office had worn shoes like that.

Joan.

I thought I was going to be sick. I ran my hands over my face as I tried to slow my racing heart. *This thing crouched in the corner can't be Joan. We all saw her carried out of the lift.*

That wasn't true, though. We'd seen *something* carried out on a stretcher, but the cloth had never been lifted. She'd had a closed-coffin funeral, too.

I wiped my hands across my eyes, smudging away tears and leaving dust in its place. *If Joan came this far before giving up…*

Her bony hands were clamped over a plain manila folder. I had a terrible premonition of what it would contain, and I leaned forward just far enough to reach it. Without disturbing Joan's body, I pulled the folder's corner back to expose the name inside:

PERRICK, Clarissa

I slumped back, resting against the concrete block, a bitter taste permeating my mouth. Cold dust billowed around me, prickling at my skin and irritating my eyes. I let out my breath in a long heave, watching it make the dust swirl.

Something on the other side of the door imitated my

exhalation. I scuttled back, my heart thumping, as something large and dark reached up to scratch at the foggy glass.

Andrew, arms crossed over his chest, listened to Thompson's speech as he leaned against Matt's desk. It had been cleared during the night.

"Yes, sadly, Matt handed in his resignation yesterday afternoon," Thompson said. He turned his head slowly to survey the gathered staff. "He was an excellent worker, and we wish him all the best in his future career. We understand it will leave a hole in this team, but we hope to hire a replacement within the week. Thank you."

The murmurs started immediately.

"I can't believe it," Madison said. "I thought he loved this job. I had no idea he was thinking about leaving."

"You know what this means, don't you?" Jacob said. "This is the sixth person who's left after an archive run. There's something not right down there. You know, during my last trip I—"

Andrew tuned out the chatter as a heavy hand landed on his shoulder. He turned to see Thompson beaming at him. "Andrew, right? I have a job for you. You see, when Matt was fetching the folders on Friday, he missed one—Clarissa Perrick. I can trust you to find it for us, can't I?"

"Sure thing."

AUTHOR'S NOTE

"Sub Basement" always stays in my mind as a first. It's not the first story I ever wrote; that honor belongs to one of the countless text documents lost decades ago to corrupted hard drives. But it was the start of my publishing journey and my first official step toward everything else.

Because "Sub Basement" is an early story, it has some rawness around its edges, but I still very much wanted to include it here. It was my answer to the question "What story do I want to tell the most?" I've asked myself that question countless times since, but it was the first, and as a result, it might be one of the purest distillations of my aesthetic.

You'll see some of my hallmarks that I got to explore more in later books: the darkness, the stairs, the sense of dread that comes from searching an unknown landscape, and, of course, the hint of something not quite natural. All these years later, "Sub Basement" still has one of my favorite concepts.

CRYPT

PART ONE

MY SLEEPY LITTLE TOWN has a few noteworthy attractions. A novelty giant plastic banana sits just within the town limits, a sad attempt to lure families into stopping on their trips upstate. We host an annual carnival that boasts not one, but *two* hayrides. And now, according to Julie Haze, we have a vampire in our graveyard.

Julie used to be pleasantly plump, but age, a diet rich in sugar and fat, and a predisposition to spending her day in her stuffed recliner left her more bulgy than curvy. Still, she maneuvered through her tiny trailer with relative ease. Her three cats were attempting to outweigh her, and, although she gladly joked about her own size, she wouldn't hear a word of criticism against her pets.

When she'd been more mobile, she'd spent her life in the village, drifting from the restaurant to the park to the café, going anywhere she could find a soul to talk to. But with a bad hip and a hundred extra pounds weighing her down, she relied on visitors to her trailer to keep her company. And she made it very worthwhile to call in for an hour.

Julie seemed to know everything about everyone and had the town's entire history stored in her brain. Through her, I'd learned a bunker had been built under the church during the war but never actually used, that the mayor's family had enough skeletons in their closets to start their own graveyard, and that the music store's owner once had a whirlwind romance with a semifamous actress.

I visited her at least once a week. Making friends had been difficult when I first moved into the tight-knit community, but Julie had embraced my company with open arms. In turn, I loved listening to her stories.

She shuffled through the trailer, tipping packaged cookies onto a plate and filling a pitcher with iced tea while the cats wove around her legs. "I'm afraid, Sara," she said, placing the snacks on the folding table between the two overstuffed armchairs beside the window, "I've told you just about all of my best stories."

I took a cookie and nibbled on its corner while Julie settled into her chair. "Maybe you can retell some of the better tales? I wouldn't mind hearing the one about the priest's cat getting stuck in the drain again."

Julie waved away my suggestion. "Don't be ridiculous, honey. I said I'm *nearly* out; the well hasn't run dry just yet. I spent all of this morning racking my brain for a good story to tell you, and I've remembered one I haven't thought about in decades."

I sat forward as Julie handed me a drink. "It's a classic, then?"

"Well, it's old, at least. And a lot of it is conjecture and guess-work, and I'm afraid you'll have to suspend your disbelief from the rafters to get through it. But I think you'll enjoy it."

Julie settled back in her chair as one of the cats leaped into her lap. Her eyes were focused on the window, where the off-white lacy curtains filtered the morning's sun and created a mosaic of shadowy patterns across her face. She was silent for a moment, seemingly to collect her thoughts, then she wet her lips and began speaking.

It started, well, it would have to be a little more than fifty years ago. The town was smaller then and not so well connected to the cities. Most people didn't have telephones, but we all had guns. A good number of wolves and bears would find their way into town, you see, and people needed a way to protect their families and livestock.

I was twelve at the time, just a few years older than Jack Suffle. The Suffles were one of the town's founding families, though there aren't any of them left anymore. Their father had died when I was a little girl, and the mother inherited his business. They were merchants—quite well off.

Jack and his younger brother, Charlie, played in the town square most days. I don't remember much about Charlie, except that he was a roly-poly little thing who tagged along after his brother every chance he had. He cried at the slightest provocation. I used to think he was a baby, but then, he *was* very young.

Jack involved himself in some insane antics. He got himself stuck in the well one time, and he very likely would have drowned if Charlie hadn't run for their mother. Jack used to brag about going into the woods on his own, too, and say he'd shot wolves the size of horses. That was a load of bull, of course, but I suppose he liked to imagine himself as the man of the house, a real hero who'd protect his mother and brother, though he frequently caused more harm than good.

On this particular day—it was winter; I remember that because I'd gotten a new coat as a gift and was showing it off— Jack and Charlie came marching through the town. Jack had a shotgun over his shoulder, which wasn't so unusual back then as it is now, and Charlie looked on the verge of tears. I asked where they were going.

"To the cemetery," Jack said, sounding so proud of himself. "Charlie and me are going to hunt the ghouls there."

I laughed, mainly to pretend that I wasn't so impressed. Most of the town avoided the cemetery, except during funerals. The area was divided into two parts: the modern section—modern in that day, at least—and an older section full of cracked head-stones and crypts. Our town was built over the ruins of a ghost town, you see. No one really knows who the original settlers were or where they came from, just that their homes had been long abandoned by the time the valley was claimed for our own town.

All of the original buildings were demolished, except for the old cemetery, which the founders left intact when creating the new graveyard beside it.

Charlie was sniffling and saying he didn't want to go, but Jack kept saying, "Go back to Mother if you're scared." Of course, the boy wouldn't. He loved Jack. Would have followed him to the ends of the earth, I imagine.

I followed with them past the town center and into the farming territory. The cemetery was a short walk into the woods, hidden from the town, so I left them there and went home. I assumed they would fool around among the gravestones for a few hours before coming back.

When I came down for breakfast the following morning, my mother told me little Charlie Suffle had gone missing. I was shocked. It felt...what's the word? *Surreal.* I remember digging my nails into the back of my hand until I drew blood because I was certain it had to be a dream. I asked what had happened, but my mother didn't know. I told her about running into Charlie and Jack before they went into the woods, and my mother said she supposed a wolf had gotten him.

You can imagine how I felt. Sad—mostly for his mother's sake—shocked, and very, very curious. Back in those days, an alley ran behind the pub, where we could wriggle into an alcove next to one of the air vents and listen to the men talking inside. All of the most important bits of news were aired in the pub. I went there as soon as I could after breakfast, but the alcove was already occupied—by Jack Suffle.

He'd been crying but was pretending he hadn't. "They don't believe me," he said before I could even open my mouth. "They think I'm making it up."

"Making what up?" I asked.

"The vampire."

I put two and two together. "Is that what got Charlie?"

Jack nodded, and though he wouldn't look at me, he beckoned for me to sit next to him. "It was in the crypt—the one in the old part, you know? I saw it first and fired my gun at it, but that just made it angry. I told Charlie to run. I thought he was behind me, but when I got to the crypt door, he wasn't there. They don't believe me. Not even mother."

He was doing an increasingly bad job of hiding his tears, and I'm afraid to say I wasn't much comfort. We sat for a while and caught snatches of conversation from inside. Men were arguing about what to do and whether they should arrange a second search of the forest. Apparently, a group had already looked for the lost boy shortly after Jack had returned home without his charge, but they had been forced to abandon the search when nightfall had made the woods too dangerous. Some of the men thought Jack had lost his brother during the walk and that there was a chance the boy was still alive in the forest. Others thought Jack may have accidentally killed him—maybe a slip of the gun or the child had fallen off a cliff—and was too ashamed to tell the truth. A third faction was in favor of believing at least part of Jack's story and searching the graveyard.

I left before the men reached a consensus, but from what I

gathered in the following days, the third faction eventually won. A half-dozen men armed with guns scoured the cemetery, paying special attention to the crypt where Jack said he'd lost Charlie. They didn't find so much as a hair from the boy's head.

Jack's mother was beside herself. She begged them to search the woods—and they did for the remaining daylight hours that day and for two days following. The woods were wild, remember. It was slow progress with just six men and Jack's mother.

On the third day, they found Charlie's body washed up on the shore of the river, quite a distance from town. He wasn't much recognizable, except for his shoes, which his mother remembered buying. They gave him a respectful burial—the carpenter had to make a special casket because the boy was so small—and agreed that it had most probably been an accidental drowning.

Jack, meanwhile, stuck to his story with the stubbornness of a mule. No, they'd gone nowhere near the river, he would say. No, Charlie didn't wander into the woods on his own. They'd gone to the graveyard, and a vampire had caught him.

Maybe things would have come out differently if people had believed—or at least pretended to believe—Jack. He was adamant and desperate for someone to take him seriously—and the town ridiculed him for it. Some of the other children found a cloak with a high collar and took turns jumping out from around corners wearing the cape and paper fangs. This went on for about a week before Jack lost it and attacked one of the children. Broke a nose and some ribs. My mother told me not to spend any time around him after that, so I really only saw him from a distance.

From what I understand, Jack's mother was patient and kind toward him, but she also believed her son had drowned in the stream. Over several months, Jack became less and less adamant about his story and started using phrases such as "I thought" and "it seemed like." He stopped exploring and became shy and withdrawn. I sometimes bumped into him at the grocers, but he never spoke to me.

By the time I was nineteen, I had almost completely forgotten about the entire ordeal. I was engaged to my husband—rest his soul—and eagerly looking forward to my wedding the following month when Jack Suffle approached me.

Since Charlie's death, the family had withdrawn from town social life. The mother, Mrs. Suffle, still ran her late husband's merchant business, but mostly by correspondence. I sometimes saw Jack in town, but he didn't seem to have friends. I'd just finished selling some of our hens' eggs to the grocer when I felt a tap on the shoulder.

"Can we have a word?" Jack asked.

I saw him so infrequently that it took me a second to remember his name. "Of course," I said then followed him out of the store and to a quiet alley.

Watching his feet, he wouldn't meet my eye. He kept opening and closing his mouth, and I was more than a little frustrated by the time he actually spoke.

"You remember the day Charlie died?" he asked.

"Yes," I said, scrambling to recall the details. He'd drowned, hadn't he?

"Do you remember talking with me behind the pub?" Jack chanced a glance at my face.

It was coming back to me quickly. "Oh, yes, you were upset because they wouldn't believe you."

"That's what I want to know. What did I tell them? What didn't they believe?"

I was becoming uncomfortable, but I answered him regardless. "You said a vampire took Charlie."

He let his breath out in a great whoosh, as though he'd been holding it for hours. "Good. Good. That's what I remember. I just…good."

I was starting to regret agreeing to talk to him, but I was too fascinated to stop myself from asking, "Didn't you remember?"

He said, "Ha!" But it wasn't a proper laugh, more of an imitation of emotion. "I thought I did, but mother says…she thinks I made it up later…I just…wanted to make sure I wasn't crazy. This has been hanging over me for so long. I think I need to confront it before I can move on, you know?"

I didn't really know. Still, I nodded to keep him happy. Jack gave me a tight smile then abruptly walked away. That was the last time I saw him.

His mother says he came home, took the gun off the wall, and left again. She didn't think anything of it, as he sometimes went out hunting when he'd finished his chores. A few of the farmers say they saw him walking to the edge of the town by the road that led to the cemetery. He never came home.

Just as they had when Charlie went missing, the townspeople

searched the woods for several days. They didn't find his body, though. After a few weeks, they held a discreet funeral for him. I attended, but not many other people did.

The popular opinion is that Jack killed himself. Charlie, his baby brother, had died while under his care, and the grief and guilt had grown stronger and stronger until he was unable to escape it. His mother believed he'd taken his own life, too. He'd brought up Charlie's death that morning, she said, during breakfast.

Everyone agreed it was a tragedy. Some thought the family was cursed with premature death. Mrs. Suffle didn't live more than a year after losing Jack. She died in her sleep. She'd had a hard life. Her husband and her two children had passed in their prime, and money can't replace family.

Well, I have a slightly different theory about what happened to Jack. I think Jack was telling the truth about the vampire. I agree that the grief of Charlie's death had been eating at him, but instead of choosing to end his life, he confronted his monster… and lost. They searched the woods, but no one thought to search the cemetery. I often wonder if they might have found his body in that big old crypt.

There's one particular reason I'm inclined to think that. No one else paid much heed to it, but that river they found Charlie in—well, it runs right past the north border of the cemetery. Yes, I think Charlie may have breathed his last in that crypt, then the monster dragged him to the river when it was done.

PART TWO

THAT WAS A VERY, very different story from what I'd been expecting to hear from Julie. I frowned at her, trying to decide if she actually believed it. She was sitting back in her chair, sipping at her tea, watching me, clearly pleased with the effect of her tale.

"And no one searched the tomb after he went missing?" I asked.

"Nope. No one seemed to think of it. The search of the woods was mainly a token gesture for his mother, really. He wasn't a precocious child anymore; he was a depressed, sullen young adult who had gone into the forest with a gun. No one had much hope of finding him alive, so they had a quiet funeral and called it a day."

I thanked Julie, finished my tea, and left her trailer. It was past midday, so I stopped in at the smallest of our town's three cafes and chewed my way through a greasy burger. I'd seen the Suffle name on a few plaques around town and assumed their family had either moved away or hadn't had any children. Knowing the tragedy Mrs. Suffle had gone through, I thought I would be less likely to overlook their monuments in the future.

Every town has tales about mythical beasts lurking just out of sight, for men to spread over a pint of beer or for children to whisper to each other during recess. I supposed the vampire was one of ours.

Still, the story niggled at me. Julie had made it sound as though Jack were approaching insanity on the day he disappeared, and the insanity had centered on the belief that a vampire had taken his brother. I didn't think it too far-fetched that he'd walked to the crypt, found it empty, then been overcome by depression and taken his life. It bothered me that no one had searched there.

I finished my lunch and began the drive home. It was a Saturday, and I didn't have anything to do except a bit of neglected housecleaning. I toyed with the idea of going to see a movie or driving to the larger library in the next town. While I was chewing over my limited options, a third, more exciting possibility snuck into my mind: *Why don't I visit Jack Suffle's crypt?*

I almost laughed at myself then thought, *Why not?*

More than forty years had passed since the events in Julie's story had taken place. Even if there was a body to find there—and that was a very big *if*—it would be a skeleton. Best case, I would have an exciting afternoon, solve a long-standing town mystery, and give Julie a new tale to tell. Worst case, I would find an empty tomb.

I turned my car toward the cemetery.

The graveyard had grown from what must have been a few dozen plots during Julie's childhood to a few hundred. A stone wall and a dense band of trees divided the old section from the new. I navigated my car down the narrow lane to the cemetery, admiring the dense pines that lined the road. Surrounded by mostly untouched natural woods, the graveyard was a few minutes' drive from the outskirts of town. It was shady under the huge trees, and the temperature felt several degrees cooler.

I parked off the road, beside the wall that surrounded the new section of the graveyard. Lichen and moss covered the wall, but it was still stable. The caretaker left the gate open during the day, so I let myself in.

A couple of the modern graves had wilting bouquets laid carefully under the headstone, and the caretaker kept them tidy and weed free. I didn't have any family or friends buried there, so I made my way through the graves at a quick pace.

The tree divider grew unchecked at the back of the cemetery, hiding the old section of the graveyard. I pushed through the shrubs and found myself facing another wall. This one was very different from the sturdy, lightly aged wall facing the road; it was taller than my head and must have been centuries old. Sections had crumbled, showing slate-gray stone under the moss and vines. There was no gate.

I paced up and down its length then eventually settled on one of the crumbled areas. Using some of the dislodged rocks as footholds, I clambered up its side, gripping vines until I could pull myself onto the top. The moss was soft and slightly slimy under my hands and would probably stain my pants. I wasn't wearing my hiking shoes, so took my time letting myself down the other side, aware that if I slipped and broke my ankle, it might take days or weeks to be found. That thought stuck in my head as my feet touched the weedy ground. Could Jack have fallen and broken a leg? He'd probably gotten in the same way I had, and he would have been hampered by his gun. I walked up and down the inside of the wall, looking for clothes or bones that might tell the story of a man's last miserable days on earth, but I found nothing.

That was a relief, at least. It would be a horrible way to go.

The old half of the graveyard hadn't been touched in decades. Dry weeds grew up to my waist in sections, and almost all of the headstones were collapsed or overgrown. Gothic statues— some of angels, some of humans, and a few that seemed to depict monsters—sprouted from the underbrush.

Julie had said the graveyard had already been there when the town was settled. I hadn't thought much about it at the time, but as I wandered among the last records of passed souls, I became aware of how strange it was that a town with nearly a hundred graves could have been so thoroughly forgotten.

I pushed the weeds away from one of the unbroken headstones and tried to make out the worn-down inscription. *Elizabeth Claireborne: Beloved mother and wife. May her soul find rest.*

Insects scurried out of the weeds and began climbing up my arms. I flicked them off with a shudder and moved farther into the cemetery.

I found the crypt from Julie's story near the back. Made entirely out of black stone, it was almost as big as Julie's trailer, but much less welcoming. Heavily weathered and a haven for weeds and spiderwebs, the doorway loomed out of the gloom like a tribute to Gothic masonry. The light penetrated no more than a few paces past the opening.

I pulled my car keys out of my pocket and pressed the button on the small LED light attached. The light was laughably weak, but it was better than being blind. I walked through the archway and took four steps before the floor disappeared.

I cried out and stumbled back, managing to catch my balance at the last moment. Shining my light at the floor showed the edge of a step, and I swallowed. What I'd assumed was the entire crypt was merely an entryway.

The steps were slimy and damp, so I took them slowly and kept my free hand pressed to the wall. My eyes slowly began to adjust as I moved deeper into the tomb and the darkness thickened, and the LED light became more useful. The walls were smooth stone, carved carefully and blemish free. Whoever had owned this crypt must have been either very wealthy or very important—or both.

I counted twenty steps before the floor leveled out. I had been expecting a single room, but the steps ended in a hallway that extended to the left and the right. Leaves, dirt, and even a few animal bones littered the foot of the steps, and the musty, stale air pushed against my eardrums as though the pressure had doubled. I peered as far as I could down both pathways, but the light was too weak to see more than a few meters. I chose left.

The path continued for twenty paces. Like the stairs, the walls were perfectly smooth. The leaves on the ground soon disappeared, leaving stone with a thin coating of dirt. The air was heavy, almost as dense as soup, and it clogged my throat. Before long, the path ended in another intersection.

I thought I might have stumbled into a subterranean labyrinth, so I chose left again, so I could retrace my steps easily if the path kept splitting. The passageway ended, however, after a dozen steps, in a square room. The room was just a few meters wide. A raised dais took up most of the room; a carved stone coffin sat on top. Intricate runes were spaced around the lid, with words carved in the center. I approached it carefully and shone my light onto the inscription:

Eleanor White
Loving mother, compassionate friend
Unlucky in marriage
May her sleep be eternal

The inscription felt unreasonably gloomy for someone's last resting place, but I supposed maybe her husband hadn't been liked. He would have been wealthy—possibly the wealthiest man in the town—to afford the below-ground temple. And, historically, the rich didn't always place well in popularity contests.

I left the room and followed the pathway straight, down what would have been the right-hand turn from the main passageway. It ended in another room that had a dais, but no coffin. I gave the room a quick search, but there was nothing to see: just smooth stone walls and floor and an empty waist-height dais.

The subterranean crypt was cold, and I pulled my jacket around myself more snugly as I retraced my steps into the main passageway and past the stairs to the outside. The leaves crunched under my feet for a dozen paces before the floor returned to being empty. I was becoming disoriented and dizzy. The thick air and the identical empty walls and floors were clouding my head and making it hard to think. The farther I walked, the more aware I became of a stench. The cloistering smell got down my throat and made me want to gag. It was musty, bitter, and dry, and it carried hints of organic decay.

For a moment, I thought it might be the smell of Jack's corpse, but he would have turned to bones a long time ago. It was more likely that an animal had gotten into the cemetery and died in a corner of the crypt.

Just as it had before, the path split. I chose left and soon found myself in a small room identical to the first, where a stone coffin rested atop a dais. I leaned over the coffin's lid, careful not to disturb the layer of dust, and read the inscription.

Christopher White
Taken in his Infancy
His mother loved him

I turned, casting my light around the room in case I'd missed something, but it was completely empty except for the coffin and a dead beetle in one corner. The smell was only slightly better than it had been in the passageway, which meant its source had to be in the remaining unexplored room.

I returned to the passageway and continued on straight. In the final hallway, I found the first signs of imperfection in the walls. If everything else hadn't been so eerily smooth, I would have missed it, but the hollow caught my eye as soon as the LED's light fell over it. The small indentation was the width of my finger, and something shiny and silver was inside…

A bullet. So, Jack was here after all…but which trip did this lodged round belong to? When Jack came with Charlie, had he accidentally shot his brother after all? Or had the second visit been the last expedition of his life?

I could see the entrance to the final room ahead. The smell was nearly overpowering, but I sucked in a breath and stepped through the doorway. It was simultaneously very similar and very different from the previous rooms. It was the same size and made of the same stone, but the walls were pocked with nearly a dozen holes. *What was he firing at?*

The coffin on the dais was not intact. The stone lid lay on the floor, cracked in three places. Dust had gathered over the toppled lid; the coffin must have been opened for a long time. I couldn't see inside.

I'd come to the old graveyard with the specific goal of finding a skeleton, but faced with the possibility of actually seeing one, all I could think of was leaving the tomb and running to my car without looking back.

Don't be a coward. It's just bones.

I approached the lip of the stone box, my heart hammering and the hairs on my arms standing on end. Images flashed through my mind: a twisted corpse, its clothes in rags, scraps of dried skin still stuck to the bleached-white bone. I squeezed my eyes half-closed as I peeked over the edge, then I let my breath out with a whoosh. The coffin was empty.

Grinning at my stupid anxiety, I gave my hands a quick shake to loosen my trembling fingers. I started to turn away from the coffin then stopped myself. It wasn't completely empty after all; as I'd turned, my light had caught something pale in the corner of the box. It looked like paper. I reached in and plucked it out with two fingers.

The sheet of yellowed, stiff, grainy parchment felt as though it could crumble in a strong breeze, so I unfolded it carefully. I squinted in the low light to read the black ink scrawled across the paper.

"By decree," I muttered to myself, trying to comprehend the challenging scrawl. "On this day, the fourteenth of March, 1879, the White family is to be interred living in their tomb, for crimes against God and against their fellow people. The council has concluded that Lord Fitzwilliam White has contrived to bargain with the dark powers to grant his flesh immortality and take on the form of the vampire. We pray his entombment will grant the town reprieve from its suffering and that the White family may eventually find forgiveness in the next life."

The paper was signed with five names, presumably the council that had written it. I shivered, feeling as though a cold wind had rushed through my clothes, and gently replaced the paper. The decree explained a few things, at least.

Julie Haze had said no one knew anything about the people who had lived there before the current town was founded. It was only an hour's drive from the next city, but the original town would have been much more isolated in 1879. It had probably been a pioneering town, settled too far away from other cities to receive supplies reliably. If it had fallen on hard times— possibly failed crops or an exceptionally harsh winter—it wasn't difficult to imagine the desperate townspeople had looked for someone to blame. Jokes would become rumors, and rumors would become truth; drowning in stress, hunger, and grief, the suffering town could have easily turned into a Salem replica... except, instead of crying "Witch! Witch!" they had screamed "Vampire!" as they carried Fitzwilliam White, his wife, and his child into the crypt.

And they'd been buried alive. For a second, I imagined what it must have felt like to be pressed into the stone coffin then watch as the unmovably heavy lid dropped into place, blocking out light and sound. I shivered again, crossing my arms over my chest, and pushed the thought out of my head.

The human sacrifice hadn't done the town much good, anyway; it had still fallen, probably succumbing to disease, or starvation, or cold. The Whites' fate was horrible, but it might have actually been merciful compared to what their peers had endured as they struggled to survive in an unforgiving and hostile landscape.

Another thought occurred to me then. I imagined two boys, one set on adventure and the other begging to go home, entering the tomb. Of course Jack Suffle would have looked into the open coffin; that sort of morbid mystery held an allure he would have found impossible to resist. He'd picked up the parchment and read it, and the word *vampire* had stuck in his mind.

Then something had happened to little Charlie on the way home. Maybe the gun had gone off accidentally or the child had slipped into the river and drowned. Either way, Charlie had died, and Jack had been unable to save him. Grief, fear, and guilt had crawled into Jack as he ran for home, and his mind had created a coping mechanism. He'd built an alternate reality based on the most memorable part of the note he'd read. *A vampire got Charlie. It wasn't my fault; I couldn't have saved him. It was a vampire.*

If he'd lived in modern times, Jack might have had a chance of being treated with therapy and counseling. Instead, he'd been ignored, ridiculed, and accused. The psychosis had taken hold, and as the years passed, it had deepened until he believed it too completely to be dissuaded.

Of course, he'd returned to the tomb to confront the vampire he was convinced existed. But instead of fighting a fictional monster, he'd found the note in the empty coffin. It might have been enough to bring up the suppressed memories of what had actually happened that day…and so he'd walked into the woods, gun in hand, unable to tolerate the truth. The depressing narrative was pure speculation, of course, but it answered the mystery of Jack's obsession and disappearance.

I turned toward the room's exit, thinking I might pay a second visit to Julie that afternoon so I could share my discovery. She would love to know the full story, though she would probably swear she'd never actually believed in the vampire, either.

As I swung my light toward the exit, it caught on something bright and reflective above the doorway. I turned my mini flashlight toward the shape, squinting to try to make it out. Two circles a little smaller than my palm hovered near the roof, shining like the reflective posts spaced along the side of the main highway. I frowned and turned my head to the side, trying to figure out what they were.

They blinked.

My back hit the edge of the coffin as I leaped away from the creature, heart in my throat. *What is that? An owl?*

It dropped from its perch with a soft thud. I stared, fixated, unable to believe what I was seeing. The creature, only vaguely humanoid and nearly as large as me, crouched on all fours. Its skin was leathery gray, just barely a shade darker than the stone walls that had disguised it so well, and its huge, owlish eyes bulged out of a smooth head. Those eyes, flashing crimson in my flashlight's pitiful light, were the only color on the creature. Its fingers were impossibly long, and its loose, wrinkled skin hung on what seemed to be little more than a skeleton. It quivered as it stared at me, and I swear I saw anticipation in its eyes.

Faster than I could have ever imagined, it sprang toward me. The frail appearance was a ruse: it gripped my shoulders in its long fingers and hauled me off-balance, slamming me to the ground. I struggled, revolted and terrified as I tried to break out of its grip, and it bit my arm just below the shoulder.

I screamed as a dozen needle-sharp teeth cut through my shirt and punctured my skin. The key ring was still clasped in my hand, so I twisted it around and stabbed the keys at the monster's head. Without the light, I couldn't see where I had hit it, but my attacker hissed in pain and released its hold, allowing me to squirm out from under it. I scrambled backward until I hit the dais.

Hot blood was running down my arm and dripping off my elbow. Fighting to keep my mind clear despite the searing pain, I fumbled to turn on the light.

The monster had retreated to the corner of the room, crouching, its huge eyes fixed on my face. It seemed wary to attack me again; the keys had cut through the skin on its head, and a flap of the gray flesh hung loose, exposing a white skull underneath.

I staggered to my feet. My breathing thin and panicky, I held the light ahead of my body like a priest warding off a demon with his cross. The beast watched intently as I stumbled in a semicircle around it, moving to get my back to the exit. Then I turned and ran.

Thankfully, the pain in my shoulder was numbing as my feet slapped on the stone floor, carrying me away from the monster. A thought hovered in my mind, terrifying me, blocking out all reasoning. *Vampire. That was the vampire.*

I glanced behind myself, shining the light over my shoulder, looking for the two reflective eyes, but the passageway was empty. My legs felt weak, so I slowed to a jog as I rounded the corner and saw the natural light coming from the stairway ahead.

The pain had almost completely subsided, and in its place, a gentle heat spread from my shoulder, radiating through my body. My thundering heart slowed, my hands stopped shaking, and I reduced my jog to a walk.

There's actually nothing to worry about, I realized as my feet crunched the leaves littering the hallway. *Yes, it was a vampire, but so what? Why did I let it scare me so badly?*

I felt tired and a little bit drunk as I reached the stairway and began to climb. My bleeding shoulder felt pleasantly warm, and my mind was going fuzzy. I thought I heard dragging footsteps from behind me, but they didn't matter anymore.

I need to rest for a bit, I decided as I lurched onto the fourth step. *I had a shock, and I'm tired, but a little rest would do me good. Just for a moment.*

The dragging sounds behind me grew louder. They were comforting, like the ocean lapping at a white-sand beach. My feet faltered on the steps, and I fell forward, hitting the stairs hard. I tasted blood in my mouth but, surprisingly, it didn't hurt.

This is nice. Maybe I'll rest here for a bit. Regain my strength before going home.

I rolled onto my back. My vision was blurry, but I thought I could see the creature crawling up the steps toward me. I smiled at it stupidly. *I wonder what its name is. Maybe it's actually Fitzwilliam White. Wouldn't that be something? I'll have to remember to tell Julie. She'll find it so funny.*

The creature's long fingers wrapped around my ankle and thigh, and it began dragging me away from the sunlight and down the stairs. Its lips were quivering with anticipation, and its lamp-like eyes bored into my face.

It pulled me off the last step, and something cool bumped my cheek. I glanced at it; it was hard to see clearly, but I thought it was one of the animal bones that littered the entrance.

The creature was strong, and it pulled me quickly, dragging me back toward its room. I was vaguely aware of how cold the stone was under my back, but I didn't mind. All I wanted was to close my eyes and let sleep take me. I could worry about every-thing else when I woke up.

The motion stopped. We were back in Fitzwilliam's room. I still held the flashlight loosely in one hand, and it gave enough diffused light to let me see the broken coffin to my right. The creature circled me twice, inhaling deeply through the slits of his nose, then nestled his face into the crook of my neck. He bit me again—I was pleased it didn't hurt at all this time—and I turned my head to give him better access as he lapped at the blood that flowed freely.

I wonder if he'll let me float down the river when he's done? I thought sluggishly as the blood drained from my body and flowed into the creature's swelling, faintly translucent stomach. *Either way, I'll have to remember to tell Julie about this. She'll enjoy it so much.*

I smiled to myself as I let my head loll to the other side. There, in the corner of the room, only visible once my discarded light fell directly onto it, was a small pile of bones. Femurs, ribs, and a cracked skull lay in a haphazard pile, throwing twisted shadows over the wall behind them.

Oh good, I found Jack Suffle, I thought as I let my eyes drift closed.

AUTHOR'S NOTE

Horror has always been my favorite genre, but I also have a secret fascination with true crime. Each year, the backlog of unsolved deaths and disappearances grows; police task forces are established to reduce them, but they're limited in what they can do and what they need to prioritize. Can they really justify dedicating a team to revisiting an eighty-year-old disappearance when there are hundreds of new missing persons each year?

Some have raised the possibility of citizen investigations to bridge that gap, people who can research local unsolved crimes, spend the hours doing the legwork when no one else can, and send anything they uncover to the police for action.

That idea—that we all have a local mystery that has gone cold, that needs someone to dig when everyone else has resigned it to the history books—is the core of this story. But what if that cold case were more than it seemed on the surface? What if the truth was something unnatural, something terrible, something better left forgotten?

Because, despite my secret love of true crime, horror is still my favorite genre.

Read on for an excerpt from

VOICES

IN THE

SNOW

Book 1 in the Black Winter series
Available now

CHAPTER 1

"EVERYTHING WILL BE OKAY." Clare leaned forward, hunched against the steering wheel as she fought to see through the snow pelting her windshield. "Don't worry about me."

The phone, nestled in the cup holder between the front seats, crackled. Thin scraps of Bethany's voice made it through the static, not enough for Clare to hear the words, but enough to let her know she wasn't alone.

"Beth? Can you hear me? It's all right."

The windshield wipers made a rhythmic thumping noise as they fought to keep her front window clear. They were on the fastest setting and still weren't helping much.

Clare had never seen such intense snow. It rushed around her, unrelenting. Wind forced it to a sharp angle. Even with snow tires and four-wheel drive, the car was struggling to get through the mounting drifts.

The weather forecast hadn't predicted the storm. Clare had been miles from home by the time the snow began. She couldn't stop. It was too dangerous to turn back. Her only choice was to press forward.

"Mar—alr—safe—"

"Beth, I can barely hear you."

"Marnie—safe—"

Even through the static, Clare could hear the panic in her sister's voice. She tightened her fingers on the steering wheel and forced a little more speed into the accelerator. "Yes. I'm on my way to get her. I'll be there soon."

That had been the plan: collect Marnie then drive to her sister's house. Beth's property had a bunker. They would be safe there, even as the world collapsed around them.

Clare had been asleep when the first confused, incoherent stories appeared on social media. She'd been in her kitchen, waiting for the coffeepot to finish brewing when the reports made it to an emergency news broadcast. She kept her TV off on Sundays. If not for Beth, Clare might have remained oblivious, curled up with a good book, and trying to pretend that Monday would never arrive.

But Beth watched the news. She'd seen the blurry, shaky footage taken just outside of London, and she had started rallying their small family. "We'll be safer together," she'd said. "We'll look after each other."

That included not just the sisters, but their aunt, Marnie. She lived on a farm an hour from Clare's house. Her only transportation was a tractor. Clare and Beth made time to visit her regularly, checking that she was all right and bringing her extra supplies when she needed them. She was the closest family they had. Now that the world was crumbling, there was no way Clare could leave their aunt alone to fend for herself.

"Op—stop—stop!" The static faded, and Beth's voice became clear. She sounded like she was crying. "Stop! Please!"

"Beth?" Clare didn't move her eyes from the road. Soon, she would be at the forest. The trees would block out the worst of the snow and give her some respite. Until then, she just had to focus on moving forward and staying on the road.

"It's too danger—s—turn ba—"

"I'm picking up Aunt Marnie." Clare flicked her eyes away from the road just long enough to check the dashboard clock. "I'll be there before noon, as long as none of the roads are closed. We'll phone you and make a new plan then."

She'd thrown supplies into the back of her car before leaving: canned food, jugs of water, and spare clothes. Worst-case scenario, she could stay at Marnie's place for a few days until the snow cleared. Marnie might not have a bunker, but Clare wanted to believe they would be safe—in spite of what the news said.

The storm seemed to be growing worse. She could barely see ten feet ahead of her car. Massive snowdrifts were forming against ditches and hills, but the wind was vicious enough to keep the powder from growing too deep on the road. Even so, her car was struggling. Clare forced it to move a fraction quicker.

She couldn't see the forest but knew it wasn't far away. Once she was inside, she would be able to speed up.

A massive, dark shape appeared out of the shroud of white. It sat on the left side of the road, long and hulking, and Clare squinted as she tried to make it out. It was only when she was nearly beside it that she realized she was looking at two cars, parked almost end to end, with their doors open.

"Dangerous—" The static was growing worse again. "Don't—as—safe!"

Clare slowed to a crawl and leaned across the passenger's seat as she tried to see inside the cars' open doors. Snow had built up on the seats. The internal lights were on, creating a soft glow over the flecks of white. In the first car, children's toys were scattered around the rear seat. A cloth caterpillar hung above the window, its dangling feet tipped with snow.

Clare frowned. There was nothing but barren fields and patchy trees to either side of the road. The owners couldn't have gone far in the snow. She hoped a passing traveler had picked them up.

Or maybe they hadn't left willingly. A surreal, unpleasant sensation crawled through her stomach. The cars' doors hung open, and the keys were still in the ignition.

She pressed down on the accelerator to get back up to speed. The steady *thd thd thd* of the windshield wipers matched her heart rate.

The abandoned cars had absorbed her attention, and she hadn't realized the static had fallen quiet. She felt for the phone without taking her eyes off the road then held it ahead of herself so that she could watch both at the same time.

The call had dropped off. Clare tried redialing. The phone hung in suspense, refusing to even try to place the call.

"Come on," Clare whispered. She pushed her car to go a little faster, even though she knew she was testing the limits of safety. Reception was bad in that area, and the storm had to be making it worse, but Beth would panic if she couldn't reconnect.

Clare tried to place the call again. And again. And again. The phone wouldn't even ring. She muttered and dropped it back into the cup holder so that she could give the road her full attention. As long as she made it to Marnie's, everything else would be all right. They would find some way to contact Beth and put her mind at rest. And if it came to it, she and Marnie could hide in her rural farm until some kind of rescue arrived.

Something small and dark darted past her car. Reflexively, she jerked the steering wheel and only just managed to correct it before the car began to spin. Clare pressed one hand to her racing heart and clenched the wheel with the other.

What was that? A fox?

It had looked too large for a fox, closer to a wolf, really, and there were no wolves in the area. It had nearly stranded her, whatever it was. She needed to focus more and not let her mind wander, no matter how much it wanted to. The family had stuck together like glue her whole life. They would find a way to stick together now.

A bank of shadow grew out of the snowstorm ahead, and

Clare sucked in a tight breath as she recognized what it meant. The forest. Safety. Shelter. She resisted the urge to go full throttle and instead let her car coast in under the massive pines.

Banksy Forest was a local curiosity. Rumors said the growth had started out as a pine plantation. Even two centuries later, from the right angle, the neat rows were visible. But no one had come to cut the trees down once they reached maturity, so they had been allowed to grow and die as they wished, only to be replaced by more pines and any other plants that managed to have their seeds blown or dropped among them.

The forest held an air of mystery and neglect in almost equal parts. It covered nearly forty square kilometers, dividing the countryside. The oldest trees were massive. Lichen crusted the crevices in their bark. The weary branches seemed to droop with age, and organic litter had built up across the ground in banks almost as deep as the fallen snow.

Clare could still hear the storm raging. But entering the forest was like driving into an untouched world. Snow made it through the treetops, but with no wind to whip at it, the flakes fell gently. The temperature seemed a few degrees warmer, and the car's heater worked a little better. Instead of looking at a screen of white, Clare could see far along the path, as if she were staring into a tunnel. The forest was deeply shaded, and she kept her high beams on but turned the windshield wipers off. She breathed a sigh of relief as the rhythmic *thd thd thd* noise fell quiet.

The government maintained the road that ran through Banksy Forest. It was a simple two-lane highway that connected

Winthrop, near Clare's cottage, and West Aberdeen, where Bethany lived. The drive through the forest took twenty minutes, and shortly after it ended, a side road would lead Clare to Marnie's house.

I can do this. The path was clear, so she allowed the car some more speed. *As long as the storm lets up before the roads are too choked. As long as there are no accidents blocking the streets. I can do this.*

She reached for the phone to try Beth's number again, but before she could touch it, a strange noise made her look up.

CHAPTER 2

CLARE TRIED TO MOVE. She felt heavy and sluggish, like weights had been attached to all of her limbs. Her head throbbed. A slow, deep ache pulsed in her right arm.

She cracked her eyes open and flinched against the light. It wasn't bright. In fact, the room she was in was deeply shadowed, but even the soft glow sent spears of pain through her skull.

Where is this? Directly above her was a plain cream ceiling. It seemed a long way away, though—higher than her roof at home. She forced her neck to tilt so that she could see to the side.

To her right was a large, dark wooden door and strange wallpaper. Marnie had cheerful fruit-themed wallpaper in her kitchen, but she was the only person Clare knew who still decorated with it. The gray pattern was definitely not Marnie's warm white-and-yellow paper. It was decadent, with flourishes and floral shapes painted over a dark-blue background. The patterns were layered, weaving over and under each other and playing tricks on her eyes.

She spread her fingers to feel the surface she was on. It was soft. *A bed.* The crisp sheets were smoother than the ones on her bed at home.

Every movement was taxing, but she turned her head to the other side. She finally found the source of the light. Two candles were placed on a dark wood, ornately carved bedside table. Their glow was soft and warm compared to the harsh white light fighting its way through the gauzy curtains across the windows.

She blinked and squinted. Between the drapes, she was fairly sure she could see snow beating at latticed windows. The storm hadn't abated. She didn't know how long she'd been out of it, but she was nowhere near her car. Or anywhere else she recognized.

The last thing she remembered was driving. *Driving where? To Marnie's? It wasn't for a regular visit...was it?*

She remembered a feeling of stress. That wasn't normal. She loved Marnie. She remembered struggling to see through the snowstorm. That was also strange. She knew better than to leave her home when the weather was like that. The risk of becoming stranded was just too great. There had been something about a phone. *Did Marnie call me? Is that why I was racing to reach her?*

She tried to get a sense of where she was. Three tall, narrow windows were spaced along the wall. Curtains diffused the long strips of cold, white light growing across the carpeted floor and up the opposite wall, where an oversized fireplace crackled. The room was huge. Every piece of furniture was made from wood and held a sense of importance. Gilded cornices. Carvings. Intricate patterns.

Something moved, and Clare's heart rate kicked up a notch. Throbbing pain pounded through her head, and she had to squint against it. A man stood near the closest window. His dark clothes had let him blend in with the drapes. He faced away from her, staring through the glass as he watched the snow fall. She couldn't see much of him. He was tall, though, and wore a jacket. His hands were clasped behind his back.

Clare held perfectly still, breathing silently to avoid drawing attention. She didn't know the house, and she didn't know the man. The word *abduction* ran through her mind, and it was hard not to feel sick at the thought of it.

Quickly, Clare. Focus. Assess.

She wriggled her toes. Even that small effort was exhausting, but her toes worked at least. Without moving her head, she glanced down at her arms, which lay on top of the bed's quilt. The right arm, the one that hurt, was swaddled in bandages from the shoulder down to the fingers. She tried flexing her hand, and the pain intensified.

She could feel more bandages on her throat, her abdomen, and her leg, but none of them hurt like her arm did.

Bandages are a good sign. You didn't bandage people you intended to kill…unless you're a sadist and don't want your victim to die too quickly.

Her throat tightened, and Clare had to force her breaths back to a slow, even state to keep them quiet. Discreetly, and moving slowly, she wormed her left arm under the covers. She felt around the bandages on her midsection. They seemed to have been applied carefully. She was wearing underwear, but the rest of her clothes had been taken off.

The man swayed as he shifted his weight from one foot to the other. She couldn't get a read on him while he was facing away from her. But he was well over six feet, and broad shoulders suggested muscles hidden under his jacket.

Damn it. Clare looked back toward the door. It wasn't far away, but its size and age made her think it wouldn't open silently. *Maybe if I had a weapon...*

She looked for anything that might give her some kind of protection. The lamps fixed to the walls would make good batons, but only if she could break them free, and she didn't know if she was capable of that. The fireside chairs and small table would be too heavy to lift. But beside the fireplace, leaning against a stack of dry wood, was a set of metal utensils, including a poker. It was on the other side of the room, which was a long way to walk without being noticed. But it was the closest thing she could see that might offer her even a shred of defense.

Moving as slowly and quietly as she could, Clare squirmed toward the edge of the bed, silently cursing every time the sheets rustled. The wind beating against the house created a soft but persistent wail, and the stranger didn't seem to hear her. She got her legs over the edge of the bed and carefully, warily sat up. A wave of dizziness washed through her, and the headache intensified. She waited. The pain receded after a moment.

The stranger shifted again, tilting his head to look at something outside. Clare held still a moment to ensure he wasn't about to turn to her, then she fixed her attention on the fire poker. She could try to creep to it, but she had less risk of being intercepted if she ran. She pictured what she needed to do: a dash across the room, use her uninjured left arm to snatch up the poker, swivel to face the stranger, and be prepared to swing if he was coming after her.

Her mouth was dry. Her legs shook. She took a final second to steel herself then leaped forward.

She took one step before her knees buckled and dropped her to the ground. Clare gasped then bit down on a scream as pain tore through her arm and her midsection. Her vision flashed white as the migraine stabbed through her head. She couldn't move. She could barely breathe.

Something large appeared at her side. The man was speaking, but her ears felt as though they had been stuffed with cotton, and she couldn't make out any words. She clutched her good arm over the injured one, begging the pain to stop and trying not to throw up.

One arm wrapped around her shoulders, then the other slipped under her knees. Everything lurched as the man lifted her off the floor. The headache worsened, and Clare pressed her lips together to keep her pained gasps inside. Then she was placed back down on something soft—probably the bed—and the presence at her side disappeared.

Slowly, the pain began to recede like a swell washing back into the ocean. Clare cracked her eyes open. The cream ceiling swam. Her breaths still came in sharp, staccato gasps, but each one felt less strained than the last.

A cold, damp cloth pressed against her forehead. That felt good. She let her eyes close. The stranger spoke to her, but she still couldn't understand him. A moment later, she felt blankets being draped back across her body.

She tried to say, "Leave me alone," but the words came out slurred. A hand pressed onto her shoulder and squeezed very lightly, then it was gone again.

ABOUT THE AUTHOR

Darcy Coates is the *USA Today* bestselling author of *Hunted*, *The Haunting of Ashburn House*, *Craven Manor*, and more than a dozen other horror and suspense titles. She lives on the Central Coast of Australia with her family, cats, and a garden full of herbs and vegetables. Darcy loves forests, especially old-growth forests where the trees dwarf anyone who steps between them. Wherever she lives, she tries to have a mountain range close by.